John Creasey – Master

Born in Surrey, England in 1908 into a were nine children, John Creasey grew up to be a true master story teller and international sensation. His more than 600 crime, mystery and thriller titles have now sold 80 million copies in 25 languages. These include many popular series such as *Gideon of Scotland Yard*, *The Toff*, *Dr Palfrey* and *The Baron*.

Creasy wrote under many pseudonyms, explaining that booksellers had complained he totally dominated the 'C' section in stores. They included:

Gordon Ashe, M E Cooke, Norman Deane, Robert Caine Frazer, Patrick Gill, Michael Halliday, Charles Hogarth, Brian Hope, Colin Hughes, Kyle Hunt, Abel Mann, Peter Manton, J J Marric, Richard Martin, Rodney Mattheson, Anthony Morton and *Jeremy York*.

Never one to sit still, Creasey had a strong social conscience, and stood for Parliament several times, along with founding the One Party Alliance which promoted the idea of government by a coalition of the best minds from across the political spectrum.

He also founded the British Crime Writers' Association, which to this day celebrates outstanding crime writing. The Mystery Writers of America bestowed upon him the Edgar Award for best novel and then in 1969 the ultimate Grand Master Award. John Creasey's stories are as compelling today as ever.

INPECTOR WEST SERIES

Inspector West Takes Charge
Inspector West Leaves Town (Also published as: Go Away to Murder)
Inspector West at Home (Also published as: An Apostle of Gloom)
Inspector West Regrets
Holiday for Inspector West
Battle for Inspector West
Triumph for Inspector West (Also published as: The Case Against Paul Raeburn)
Inspector West Kicks Off (Also published as: Sport for Inspector West)
Inspector West Alone
Inspector West Cries Wolf (Also published as: The Creepers)
A Case for Inspector West (Also published as: The Figure in the Dusk)
Puzzle for Inspector West (Also published as: The Dissemblers)
Inspector West at Bay (Also published as: The Case of the Acid Throwers)
A Gun for Inspector West (Also published as: Give a Man a Gun)
Send Inspector West (Also published as: Send Superintendent West)
A Beauty for Inspector West (Also published as: The Beauty Queen Killer)
Inspector West Makes Haste (Also published as: Murder Makes Haste)
Two for Inspector West (Also published as: Murder: One, Two, Three)
Parcels for Inspector West (Also published as: Death of a Postman)
A Prince for Inspector West (Also published as: Death of a Assassin)
Accident for Inspector West (Also published as: Hit and Run)
Find Inspector West (Also published as: Doorway to Death)
Murder, London - New York
Strike for Death (Also published as: The Killing Strike)
Death of a Racehorse
The Case of the Innocent Victims
Murder on the Line
Death in Cold Print
The Scene of the Crime
Policeman's Dread
Hang the Little Man
Look Three Ways at Murder
Murder, London - Australia
Murder, London - South Africa
The Executioners
So Young to Burn
Murder, London - Miami
A Part for a Policeman
Alibi (Also published as: Alibi for Inspector West)
A Splinter of Glass
The Theft of Magna Carta
The Extortioners
A Sharp Rise in Crime

Strike for Death

(The Killing Strike)

John Creasey

Copyright © 1958 John Creasey
© 2014 House of Stratus

All rights reserved. No part of this publication may be reproduced, stored in a retrieval system, or transmitted, in any form, or by any means (electronic, mechanical, photocopying, recording, or otherwise), without the prior permission of the publisher. Any person who does any unauthorised act in relation to this publication may be liable to criminal prosecution and civil claims for damages.

The right of John Creasey to be identified as the author of this work has been asserted.

This edition published in 2014 by House of Stratus, an imprint of Stratus Books Ltd., Lisandra House, Fore Street, Looe, Cornwall, PL13 1AD, U.K.
www.houseofstratus.com

Typeset by House of Stratus.

A catalogue record for this book is available from the British Library and the Library of Congress.

ISBN 07551-3640-3
EAN 978-07551-3640-7

This book is sold subject to the condition that it shall not be lent, resold, hired out, or otherwise circulated without the publisher's express prior consent in any form of binding, or cover, other than the original as herein published and without a similar condition being imposed on any subsequent purchaser, or bona fide possessor.

This is a fictional work and all characters are drawn from the author's imagination. Any resemblance or similarities to persons either living or dead are entirely coincidental.

Chapter One

Incitement to Strike

Tessa lee felt almost frightened as she watched the crowd; and was fascinated by the man who stood on the box, waving his arms and mouthing words she could not hear because the office window was closed. Even if she opened it she would catch only a word here and there, and she was not sure that she wanted to hear what he said.

She had only seen him a few times, and then casually; now she felt that she hated him.

A watery spring sun broke through clouds, and shone on his reddish hair, glinted on his rimless glasses. Then he said something which amused the crowd of workers, she saw their faces break into grins, could imagine the laughter. Two or three elderly men in overalls turned from the edge of the crowd of over a thousand strong, and walked towards the factory gates. Tessa, watching them, thought that they looked worried. The smiling and the laughter ceased. She saw a new change in the expressions of the men, and suddenly there was a kind of commotion. Some waved and shouted in unison, making a sound which came faintly through the window; it seemed to Tessa that it was the sound of a mob, roaring. Silence and stillness fell.

Then laughter shook them all again. The red-haired man had humoured and delighted them.

Two things happened, one quick upon the other, to draw the girl's attention from the orator and the crowd. She heard the handle of the door turn; and in the distance saw a car come into sight along the road which led to the factory from the main road. She glanced round, and saw Mr Cobb, secretary to Munro Motors, silvery-haired although he was not yet fifty, a small, precise, neat-looking man whom one had to know for a long time before liking.

Tessa had known him for six years, since she had first come to work at Munro's, and wasn't sure yet whether she liked him or not.

He smiled, thinly, as he approached with some papers in his hand.

"So you've been watching, too, Miss Lee."

"I couldn't help myself."

"I don't think anyone could." Cobb put the papers down on Tessa's desk, near the typewriter, and looked out of the window, frowning, obviously perturbed. "I'm afraid they're coming out this time."

"But it's so crazy!"

"It may look crazy," Cobb said. "I never really know." His gaze moved into the near distance, so that he could see the car, a maroon-and-grey Rolls-Bentley, moving slowly towards the factory gates and the great crowd which was just inside. "I never really know," he repeated. "You see how foolish the best of people can be."

Tessa felt sure what he meant.

He would not allow himself to voice criticism of the other directors or the management in her hearing, but there could not have been a worse moment for Malcolm Munro, the newest and youngest member of the Board, to come flaunting his luxury car. In twenty minutes' time, when the men were back at work, he could have come purring in, without attracting much attention, but now the crowd would have to move away for him, and undoubtedly some would resent it

The gates were open. A few youngsters and girls were walking on the tatty grass patch beyond, most of them in couples; the lunch-hour break gave time for snatches of romance. The sun went behind the clouds, lazily. The Rolls-Bentley came through the gates and near the crowd of workers, and judging from the way several looked round and then opened their mouths, they shouted to the others. Abuse? The red-haired man on the box didn't stop speaking, and most of the men were too interested in what he had to say to take any notice of those on the fringe.

The Rolls-Bentley was forced to a standstill only a yard or two from the crowd.

Tessa could see Malcolm at the wheel; alone.

He wound the window down and spoke to someone nearby, a man who nodded and moved off. More men called out. Most of them, their backs to the car, had no idea that it was there, but the speaker knew because he was facing it. He took no notice, and seemed intent on holding the crowd enthralled; and so holding up the junior director.

"You see what I mean," said A. C. Cobb, in his thin voice. He looked straight at Tessa, surprising her by his frankness. "Mr Munro must have known that the meeting was to be called today, and yet he comes at the worst possible moment. Then Grannett tries his strength and stops the crowd from moving, so one thing sets off another. If you judged from this kind of occurrence you would think that management and men were implacable enemies, but each of these is a worthy man, and over a drink they would be perfectly good friends."

Then he caught his breath.

Tessa had been looking at him, but at the look of horror in his expression swung round towards the window again. She was in time to see the missile in flight, although she didn't see who threw it. It looked like a darkish ball, curving through the air; it fell plumb on the roof of the Rolls-Bentley, and split into a yellowy, squashy mess.

Tessa could see now that it was an orange.

Juice must have splashed very close to Malcolm.

"Oh, the *fools*," groaned A. C. Cobb.

Tessa almost prayed. 'Malcolm, don't lose your temper, don't—'

He was thrusting open the door of the car, a lithe, tanned, good-looking man in the late twenties, a fine athlete, a top-class amateur boxer, reckoned a good sort in most circles, but little more than a beginner at Munro's. Hatless, his dark hair blew about in the wind, wiry and difficult to part. As he stood up by the side of the car and called out something which Tessa couldn't hear, a second orange smacked against the pillar of the door.

Tessa felt a helpless, hopeless kind of dismay.

As the orange smacked squashily, and before he felt the spattering mess, Malcolm Munro realised that he was doing the wrong thing. But it had started now, and if he drew back he would give the impression that he was funking the issue. Juice and pulpy bits splashed on to his head, his face, his clothes, and a piece of peel actually lodged between his lips, so that he had to spit it out. The moment of reason disappeared, as if it had never been. He gritted his teeth and clenched his hands tightly by his side, glaring about him, unaware of the other tensions. He heard a man call out: "That's enough, don't—"

Then the voice broke off.

Another orange hurtled towards the car, but this time Malcolm saw it leave the hand of a youth of eighteen or so, on the fringe of the crowd.

The orange went wide.

Afterwards, Malcolm realised that the miss gave him a chance which he would never have again; a chance to laugh at the young fool, to ridicule him for missing at twenty yards' range. He would never know whether he would have had the crowd with him, if he had tried.

At the moment, he felt only that searing, ungovernable rage.

"I want that man," he said harshly. "That man who threw the oranges. Send him here."

The red-haired man who had been haranguing the crowd was silent now, his grip on their attention loosened. He was staring this way; so was everyone, heads or bodies twisted to do so. A few men and girls jumped up on to the wire fence, and some on to barrels of oil and paint, to get a better view.

The youth who had thrown the orange wore a khaki polo-neck sweater, and had untidy brown hair and rather a large nose. There was a scared look in his eyes.

"Come on, what's your name?" Malcolm strode forward, and the men nearer him gave way. He was a boss and they were the workers, even if they had just decided to deliver a strike ultimatum to the management; so they deferred to him. Someone nearly out of range said: "Damned young fool."

Him, Malcolm?

Or the youth?

The youth was looking right and left, as if seeking a way out. Two or three others, about the same age, were lining up in front of him, almost protectively; others gave him a wide berth. There was a moment of silence before the man on the box called out in a carrying voice: "What's going on there?"

Malcolm didn't look round at him, but pushed on through the crowd. The youth with untidy hair and the scared look was over two yards away, and still protected by three others, one of them short, stocky, red-haired, young.

Malcolm reached the party.

"Now, let's have your name," he said curtly, "and then you can go and get your cards. You're finished here."

"Take it easy, take it easy." That was the red-haired youth, who stood squarely in front of the orange-thrower, proving half a head shorter. There was nothing even remotely nervous in his manner, he was much more relaxed than anyone else nearby. "He didn't throw anything."

"You keep out of this." Malcolm was within arm's reach of the orange-thrower. "What's the matter with you? Lost your tongue?"

"I—I—I—"

"I told you he didn't do anything," repeated the redhead. "Who the hell do you think you are, throwing your weight about like this?"

"Another word out of you, and you can get your cards, too," Malcolm rasped.

Then he was jostled from behind.

He could not save himself, and staggered towards the redhead. He saw the glint of satisfaction in a pair of greenish grey eyes, a positive grin on the fine, full lips. The grin warned him what to expect. As he fell, the youth drove his fist towards Malcolm's stomach, a short arm blow that would have winded Malcolm if it had landed squarely. The split second of warning saved him. He dropped his right hand

and took the blow on his wrist. The move surprised the young redhead, who struck out with his left for Malcolm's chin.

Someone cried almost wailingly: "Stop it, can't you? Stop it!"

But his words were drowned.

The factory hooter screeched notice that it was five minutes to two, time for the men to start back to the factory workshops. It drowned the man's voice too. It drowned the young redhead's words, but undoubtedly he was swearing viciously at Malcolm, who had taken the blow glancingly on the chin. Then the hooter stopped, and the redhead's last words sounded clear and loud: "… high and mighty tricks with me, I'll smash your face in."

He looked as if he meant it.

A middle-aged man put a hand on his shoulder, but he shook it off, and squared up in front of Malcolm, face scarlet, eyes blazing, lips parted.

"Come on, put your fists up! Let's see if papa's boy has any guts!"

It was 'papa's boy' that really robbed Malcolm of the last vestige of self-control, and sent him blindly forward. He took a blow on the side of the jaw and another on the chest, but after that it was slaughter. The youth might be strong, but he didn't know a single boxing trick. When he realised what was happening to him he fell back hastily, and tried to cover up. But he wasn't frightened.

Soon, his nose and lips were bleeding and his right eye swelling. He pitched backwards, suddenly. By then, three or four men were pulling at Malcolm. He did not shake them off, but stood practically unmarked, gasping, fists still clenched, glaring at the other youths now bending over their friend; the orange-thrower was standing on one side, looking much more scared than the redhead had. He began to move forward.

"I—I'm sorry, sir, I—I didn't mean—" He swallowed his words. "I didn't—"

Then Malcolm Munro made his worst mistake of the afternoon.

"Just go and get your cards." He turned away, shrugged off the men's hands, and went back to the Rolls-Bentley. He got in, and found his hand sticky with orange juice which had been on the door handle. He was still breathing very hard, his jaw smarted a little at one side, and the knuckles of his right hand were painful. The crowd was farther away now, only one or two couples stood near the Rolls-Bentley, and they were hurrying. A dozen or so people stood by the fallen youth and his friends, and among them was the redheaded soapbox orator, Grannett, the strike advocate.

Malcolm began to tremble from reaction.

He mustn't show it. He must not betray any sign of weakness. If any good was to come out of this, it would be from a display of strength. The fallen youth was being helped to his feet, and his friends went off with him, one of them with an arm round his waist. No one looked back now, except Grannett.

He came striding towards Malcolm, a man in the early thirties, broad, stocky, powerful. The wayward sun came out again and glinted on his rimless glasses and made his head seem massive. Malcolm saw him clearly when he was twenty feet away, and realised that he was remarkably like the youth whom he had just fought.

And both had bright red hair.

This man reached the window.

Malcolm made himself say: "Well?"

"I just thought you would like to know that you've made it almost impossible to avoid a strike," he said, and his eyes were cold and accusing. "You won't have a man or girl against it until you've made a full apology for that assault. I've been waiting a long time to see a Munro make a fool of himself, and it's been worth waiting for. You'll be lucky if you're not charged with assault."

Chapter Two

Board Meeting

It was crazy to be in love with Malcolm, but there was nothing Tessa could do about that. She had expected him to go straight into his own office after the fracas, not to come through hers. Instead, he arrived only five minutes after A. C. Cobb had left, when she was putting a letter heading into the typewriter. She sat sideways to the window and facing the door, and when the handle turned her heart leaped; when she saw him come in it beat very fast indeed.

He nodded, closed the door, and came forward. She had an odd impression: that he looked older. There was a slight swelling on the left side of his chin, but she saw nothing else wrong, except that dark spots and pieces of orange dotted his pale-grey suit which fitted so perfectly, and his dark, wiry hair. His wine-red tie was badly spotted, too.

Tessa just sat and looked up at him, unable to bring herself to speak normally, and when he realised this, Malcolm looked down at her and gave a twisted smile.

"So you know what happened?"

"I saw most of it through the window."

"I didn't realise I had a wider audience." He glanced out, and she saw him clench his fists as he stood with his back to her. "The office canteen windows are on this side, too. I'll bet they had fun." He swung round on her. "Did you?"

She said: "I hated every second of it."

The glitter went out of his eyes, and he moved and sat on the corner of a low filing-cabinet which was within hand's reach of Tessa.

"Yes, you would. Thank you, Tessa. I'm not asking, I'm just wondering what you hated most: the sight of a director being stoned with oranges, as it were, or Grannett inciting the men to strike, or me making an utter fool of myself."

Tessa didn't answer.

"Well, there's one good thing, the Board's due to meet at half past three, so we needn't let the world wait in suspense," Malcolm went on. "Anyone telephoned apologies?"

"No, sir," she said.

He leaned forward until their faces were very close, and he bunched his hands tightly, as if he didn't want to move them and so touch her.

"Listen," he said gruffly, "there is a time and a place for everything, and this isn't the time or place for you to call me 'sir'. When the others are about, and that only for the time being, we have to put up with it. But when we're alone it's Tessa and Malcolm."

He broke off, and stood up abruptly.

"My day for saying the wrong thing," he said jerkily. "It has now occurred to me that you may no longer wish to call the junior director by his first name."

"Malcolm," Tessa said, very quietly, "even if you did mishandle the situation out there, it isn't the end of the world, and it isn't the first time a mistake's been made. If that boy hadn't started to throw oranges it would never have happened."

"If I hadn't been wearing the tie which you gave me for my birthday it might never have happened, either," he said, "so that way it's your fault. This is the time for facing blunt facts. I made a bloody fool of myself. I did it because I lost my temper, and when a Munro loses his temper, it's hell to pay. Do you know what Michael Grannett said? He said that he had waited a long time to see a Munro make a fool of himself, and it had been worth waiting. He's probably right." When Tessa didn't speak, Malcolm went on in a hard voice: "This is the very time when we cannot afford a strike.

The Board knows it, even I know it, and Grannett and the other shop stewards and the workers know it. Bless their little hearts, that's why they've chosen this moment to put in the demand for a ten per cent increase, and that's why they'll get it. And that's why the fact that the boy started the fight will be glossed over, and why the junior director will be expected to apologise for hitting a worthy working man who was also an insolent young pup. Like me. This is also where the junior director will have lost all respect that the factory staff and workers ever had for him, and where he writes *finis* to his promising career as the great industrial baron. How was I, while I lasted?"

"Don't talk for the sake of talking," Tessa said. "It isn't anything like as bad as that."

"It is, you know," said Malcolm. "I wonder who paid for those oranges." He moved towards the door to his office, opened it, and went on: "I can't change, I'll have to face the Board in battledress. At least I'll know I've one friend in court, you'll be on duty, as Topsy's away with that heaven-sent 'flu. When drawing up the minutes, go easy on the actual phrasing of the condemnation of the folly of Malcolm Munro, won't you? "

"They'll send me out of the room, and discuss it privately," Tessa said.

"Not if I know my father," Malcolm declared, and went in and closed his office door.

He was probably right.

He was also showing a new side to himself, one which Tessa hadn't really suspected to be present: the courage to face up to a situation and to admit that he had been wrong. A kind of bitter humility. It wasn't surprising that he blamed himself so much, and it didn't greatly matter. He was talking nonsense about resigning, of course, it wouldn't come to that.

Would it?

Tessa could not put the possibility out of her mind as she busied herself getting the agenda ready, then going to the board room across the passage, and placing the blotting-paper, the pens, pencils, pads, agenda sheet, and other documents in front of each director's chair.

There were four directors, named on the agenda:

Sir Ian Munro, Chairman
Mr Robert Amory, Managing Director
Mr Malcolm Munro
Mr A. C. Cobb, Secretary

But the agenda did not say that Sir Ian owned forty-nine per cent of the shares, and was the virtual dictator of Munro's. Yet he could be out-voted on the Board, and occasionally was.

Tessa would sit at Cobb's side, with the chairman on her other side, because he often wanted her to take notes for him, and he liked to supervise her work; in fact, everyone's work. She finished the preparations and went back to her office, and as she did so the bell from Malcolm's room rang. She picked up her pencil and pad and hurried in, but he stopped her at the door.

"Check on young Grannett, sweet, and find out how he is, will you?"

"Who?" she asked, in surprise.

"Young Grannett. Michael Grannett's brother. My victim."

"Is *that* who it was?" Tessa was genuinely aghast.

"If a job's worth doing, it's worth doing well," said Malcolm wryly. "If I'd done the right thing I would have made it Michael Grannett, that would really have fried the bacon. Let me know how the victim is, will you?"

"Yes, of course," Tessa said, then saw the handle of the outer door turn. A moment later Sir Ian Munro, *the* Munro, the only surviving founder member of the Board of Munro & Company Limited, Makers of Quality Cars, entered Malcolm's office. At the best of times he had an aggressive manner and a hostile expression, and as far as Tessa could judge now, he was in a much worse mood than usual. Probably he had been told what had happened.

She heard him say: "What's this I hear?" in his deepest, roughest voice.

She closed the door.

Before telephoning the works hospital, where all injuries both major and minor were treated, she went to the board room again and made sure that everything was ready; the water had to be taken in at the last minute, Mr Amory had an obsession about fresh water. There were a few specks of dust at A. C Cobb's place, and she blew these off, then went back to her desk and lifted the telephone.

"The hospital, please."

"Yes, Miss Lee." There was a moment's pause; then: "I'm sorry, Miss Lee, it's engaged. Shall I call you?"

"Yes, please." Tessa rang off, took her handbag from a desk drawer and the mirror out of her handbag, and studied her reflection. She looked all right; right enough to attract Malcolm, right enough to have made him say, only two nights ago, that she was so beautiful she was driving him crazy. She was the crazy one, for wanting to believe him.

There were a few letters from the morning's dictation still to be done. She rattled them off, knowing what to say almost by heart, and able to imagine Malcolm's quiet voice as he dictated, able to remember the way he looked at her. At least he played fair, didn't squeeze her or kiss her in the office, didn't make the *affaire* even remotely sordid. *Affaire?* She remembered the day she had first met him, only a year ago. His uncle, whose place he had taken on the Board, had been her boss then: Mr Paul Munro. Even at the time, she had known that the old man was ill and likely to retire, although she hadn't suspected that he would die so suddenly.

She remembered the glint and smile in Malcolm's eyes at that meeting, and the unfeigned admiration in them. His father had said, in hearty jest, that when he took over the directorship his luckiest break would be taking over the director's secretary with it,

"I couldn't agree more," Malcolm had said.

They'd all laughed.

If only Paul were alive to face this situation, instead of Sir Ian …

Tessa finished the letters and put them in the folder for signing; now there was only filing that she need do until a summons from the directors. It was three o'clock. Odd that she hadn't yet been put through to the hospital. She was tempted to ring again, but a messenger from the accounts department came in with some files and figures for the meeting, so she didn't. She found herself thinking more about Malcolm. He had been abroad much of his life, and had never intended to come into the business. A year ago, when he'd been persuaded by his father to succeed Paul Munro, it had been intended that Malcolm should spend a few months in the different departments before joining the Board, but Paul's sudden death had brought him on the Board at once. If he'd had the experience, perhaps this afternoon's bother would not have happened. The odd thing was that Malcolm had nothing of his father's impatience or intolerance. The workers were 'the chaps' to him; several had fought in his unit with him in Korea and later served in Germany with him. The internal telephone bell rang.

"Mr Malcolm's office … Oh, yes, please, put me through." They had an internal exchange, not an automatic system, one of the things Malcolm had said that he would like to put right soon. "Hallo, is Sister Marsh there? … Oh, Eileen, it's Tessa. Do you know how the man Grannett is, the one who was in a fight? "

"Yes, I do," said Sister Marsh in a rather abrupt way; she wasn't usually abrupt, least of all with her friends. "He's on his way to the town hospital now, he's much more seriously injured than we'd realised."

"Oh, no!"

"I think you'll have to find a way of making sure that boss of yours keeps his fists to himself," Eileen said, almost angrily. *"And* his temper, too. He must have gone mad."

"Eileen, young Grannett isn't really badly hurt, is he?"

"It wouldn't surprise me, but I shan't know until they've taken the X-ray," Eileen said. "It fooled me, I didn't realise how nasty it was." Her manner softened, and she went on: "No need for you to worry about it, though, but I'm afraid it's going to cause a lot of trouble in the factory. Several people have—" Her voice became brisk again. "I mustn't stop to gossip, Tessa, there are two girls outside who've cut their fingers badly, and a man's fallen down some steps, I think he's broken his collarbone. See you later."

"Yes, all right," said Tessa. "Thanks."
She felt frightened, for Malcolm.

Then the members of the Board began to arrive, looking in to announce themselves, and Tessa had no chance to tell Malcolm what she had heard. She wasn't sure that it would be wise to yet, anyhow. When she saw him next, he was very pale. There was a glitter in his eyes which she didn't like; the kind which suggested that he would soon lose his temper. His vicious temper! There must have been a scene between him and Sir Ian. She fully expected to be told that she wasn't wanted for the beginning of the meeting, but she was wrong.

Sir Ian, short, stocky, balding, had the look of a hard spirits drinker, but that was misleading. In his habits he was temperate, and he put on weight with a rapidity which made dieting necessary; his regular concessions to this problem were to take saccharin instead of sugar, and brown bread instead of white.

There had been a time, many years ago, when he had gone among the workers, knowing many by their Christian names. But as Munro Motors had grown, and the payroll had increased, that had become impossible. Now he knew very few of the men personally. In those old days he had been a generous and benevolent employer. Today, he seemed to see the employees as a kind of enemy, ready at all times to attack, demanding more than the plant could afford.

Robert Amory, tall, always a little tentative, successfully hiding the fact that he was an able managing director, was a particularly good public-relations man; undoubtedly it was Amory who had managed to keep relationship between the management and workers reasonably sweet in days when tensions had been increasingly taut in the industrial world.

A. C. Cobb was a kind of walking accounting machine, who handled not only the accounts but all the firm's statistics. He would be a little impatient with Tessa, probably, because his own secretary was away; he was always happier when Topsy Wareham was present to take notes; Topsy was the world's best note taker.

A.C. was human, though; as he'd already shown today.

There was not a great deal of ordinary business. Minutes were read, a few formal matters were discussed, and then came the main purpose of the meeting, the wage demand for a ten per cent increase; that was really why the meeting had been called. As the previous items were crossed off the agenda and the way cleared for this one, Tessa felt her own tension rising.

They would surely send her out now.

"Miss Lee, don't make any notes until I tell you," Sir Ian ordered. He sat erect in his chair, rather like the painting of him in the main entrance hall downstairs. He coughed; a nervous habit "No need to waste words. We know that the situation has been seriously aggravated by what happened at lunchtime." He looked challengingly at Cobb and Amory, but not at Malcolm; probably he had said all that he intended to say to his son. No one spoke. "Situation as I see it has changed," Sir Ian said. "We've had one of the workers deliberately throw missiles at a director, seen others protect that worker. Sharp disciplinary action must be taken if we are to preserve the position of and respect for the Board. Time has come to make it clear that we do own the plant, and are not prepared to be dictated to by any section of the employees. My recommendation is that we reject the wage increase demand outright. Any other course will be construed as weakness, and we cannot afford to be considered weak."

He stopped, breathing heavily through his wide nostrils.

Cobb, with his little pale face and rather tired eyes, looked nervous and worried. Malcolm sat almost as erect as his father, one hand resting on the big, shiny board room table. The challenge, if it came, would come from Amory, who always gave the impression that he was going to evade an issue, and always surprised Tessa by facing it with remarkable calm.

"I don't think we can do it, Mr Chairman," he said mildly.

"Nonsense. Can and will."

"If we reject it absolutely, they'll be out tomorrow."

"They'll come back fast enough."

Sir Ian must have expected this opposition, but didn't find it palatable. He was glaring at Amory's round, tentatively smiling face;

Amory's expression seemed half apologetic. "Things in the labour market aren't so rosy as they were. Had to happen sooner or later. We can't be dictated to. It's well known that we are bursting with export orders for the Mark 9 model, and that we've cut export prices to the bone to reach it. Even a five per cent wage increase would pare profits down to next to nothing, ten per cent would cause a loss. Got to be realists. Got to realise that we are doing a public service. We've been working for two years on the Mark 9, we've now got something that will sweep the Continent and America. Put a year's output behind us, add the production economies we can make in a year and we can listen to demands. To hell with their *demands,* anyhow! What right have they to demand anything? Their *request* for a rise. We can't afford it now. We must tell them so. Their representative wants his reply by five o'clock, doesn't he, Bob?"

"Yes," said Amory, and looked even more apologetic "Mr Chairman, we won't sweep any market with Mark 9 if we aren't making them."

"Strike'll be over in a week."

"I don't think you're right," argued Amory. He looked at Cobb, whose small chin seemed to shrink inside his stiff collar. "What do you think, A.C.?"

Cobb shot a worried glance at the Chairman.

"Determined mood," he said. "Distinct impression, very determined." He glanced almost fearfully at Malcolm. "Even before this afternoon's incident"

"Exactly," said Sir Ian, and banged the table, but surprisingly lightly. "They've been intractable for a long time. The moment we get our heads above water, they try to drag us down again. We've got to face this challenge. The attitude of the men towards a director proves conclusively that they are in an antagonistic and hostile mood, but they won't be so hostile when they're not getting any pay packets. I know they'll strike, I don't need telling that, but I say it will soon be over, and that the atmosphere will be much clearer. *And* cleaner. You've used the velvet glove too long, Bob. You've let the man Grannett twist you round his little finger. This proves beyond doubt that he's a dangerous man, without the interests of the company at heart. I see no alternative but to reject the de—the request. We must. If you want to sugar the pill, tell 'em we'll consider it again in six months' time. Tell 'em if Mark 9 is a success—"

"That won't help, you know," Amory said.

"It'll look good in the newspapers."

Unexpectedly, Amory laughed.

"Our export sales figures in a year's time would look better, Mr Chairman! Do you mind if I say that I think you're making a mistake in confusing two issues? The incident outside is one thing, the wage application quite another."

"Inextricably mixed up," Sir Ian declared, with very great emphasis.

When he stopped, no one spoke.

Malcolm hadn't yet uttered a word. He was still as pale as when he had come in, and Tessa knew that he was afraid that if he spoke he would lose his temper. She did not know whether to hope that he would keep silent, or whether he should say what he thought: what *did he* think, anyhow?

Then Amory looked at him, and said: "It looks as if you have the deciding vote, Malcolm. I shall vote for offering seven and a half per cent increase, on the proposal I've already put in, and the Chairman will vote against it. What do you intend to do?"

Tessa felt as if she could not breathe; the others felt the tension, too. But it was not long-lived.

Malcolm said briefly: "I shall vote for your proposal."

His father swung towards him, angry and incredulous.

"I thought I told you—"

"Mr Chairman, you may have my resignation any time you like after this meeting, but while I remain a member of this Board I shall vote as I think right, and not because I get instructions from you or anyone else," Malcolm said formally. "I shall vote for an offer of seven and a half per cent."

"I tell you to offer any increase now will be a sign of abject weakness," Sir Ian cried. "I utterly refuse to agree!"

The ringing of the telephone bell startled him so much that he broke off and glared at the instrument, which was in front of Tessa.

In the momentary hesitation which followed, all of them looked at it, and so seemed to be looking at her. An interruption at a Board meeting was one of the rare things, and could only herald news of exceptional importance.

"Well, see who it is," Sir Ian said at last, staring back at his son.

Tessa took off the receiver.

"The board room," she announced.

A man said: "Is that Miss Lee? ... This is Colonel Harrison, Miss Lee, let me speak to Mr Amory, please."

Harrison, the Works Manager, was breathing hard. Tessa did not like the note in his voice, he was seldom so abrupt or harsh. His words had sounded faintly in the room, and Amory was already stretching out for the telephone.

He took it from her.

"Hallo, George," he said. "What's on? ... Yes, of course we are." He stopped speaking, and caught his breath. His red, round face drained of its colour. Tessa shot a glance at Malcolm, and saw how startled he looked. Then Amory spoke into the telephone again, while the others watched with increasing tension. "Are you positive? ... Well, yes. Yes, of course, they'll have to be given all the help possible, but George, just a moment. I think we ought to have a pathologist to advise us, we must be absolutely sure of the cause of death as soon as possible ... We can do that through the hospital, surely ... Well, do it if you can. Yes ... Thanks." He rang off.

It was almost an anticlimax when he said: "Young Grannett died on the operating-table."

And all four of the others in the room stared at Malcolm.

Chapter Three

A Job for West

That afternoon, at a little after four o'clock, Chief Inspector Roger 'Handsome' West of New Scotland Yard was reading through a report on a trial which was being held at the Old Bailey. He was both marvelling at and confounding the brilliance of defending counsel, who might succeed in getting a guilty man off from a charge of robbery with violence.

Roger was alone in the Chief Inspectors' office, with its five biliously yellow desks, the smouldering coal fire, the green armchairs, and the battery of telephones. His desk was near the window and farthest from the door; the best position in the room, and the least draughty when the windows were open, as they were now. A few spots of rain spattered the glass. The river, just in sight, was rippled with the wind, but the water looked as clear as that of a mountain stream; that didn't fool him.

A telephone on his desk rang. His movement to lift it was automatic

"West speaking ... Oh, yes, Joe ... I'll come right along, what's on? ... That's all right, provided it isn't trouble."

He put the receiver down and stood up, a tall, powerful-looking man in the early forties, with fair hair which hid the coming grey, and almost with a film star's looks. The most noticeable thing about him was that he looked human; as if he could smile easily. His movements were brisk, suggesting energy kept on a leash. He let the door swing to behind him, and thrust open the door of a sergeants' room, next to this, and said: "Send someone in, will you?" and went on, knowing that one or two sergeants would stand in until one of the CIs got back.

All he knew was that there was a 'job out at Elling, bit different from usual'. Joe Knightley, recently promoted to senior superintendency at the Yard, always liked being a little mysterious.

His office was along the passage, a small one, with only two desks: his and a Chief Inspector's. For once, Roger entered with a feeling almost of envy. In the general promotional moves which had been made in the past six months, when Superintendents like Cortland, Abbott, and others had retired, and others had replaced them, he had been passed over; yet he was next in running for an office of his own according to length of service as a CI, if not on age.

The bad moment soon passed.

Knightley was sitting behind his large pedestal desk, a slow-moving, ponderous type of man, who did nothing without thinking three times about it. He was signing letters, nodded and motioned to a chair, then finished signing and looked up.

"Hallo, Handsome, got a good one for you, this time, one where you've got to mind your p's and q's."

"Sounds like a politician, high society, or big business," Roger said.

"Too clever, that's your trouble, too clever by half," said Knightley, without a change of expression; he had large features and rather big pores. "You want to let other people be right sometimes, Handsome. It's big business."

"Really big?"

"Big enough to have the Divisional boys ask us to send someone pronto, and the Assistant Commissioner to assign you," Knightley said. "It's out at Munro Motors plant. Don't know the rights of it yet. Some say it's to do with a strike, some say it's not. Anyhow, one of the directors got mixed up with one of the factory hands, and there was a fight. The factory hand died in hospital. That makes it manslaughter, and it could even be murder. You're to go out and have a look round, and be very careful how you deal with these people."

"It's a new one all right," said Roger, pondering. "Did I get it straight? A director and a factory hand were mixed up in a fight?"

"That's it."

"I'd like to meet that director!"

"That's just what you're going to do," Knightley said, and for the first time he grinned. "Take a sergeant, shouldn't think you'd need anyone else yet. The Divisional chaps are on the spot, and one of the works' detectives is old Charley Coombs. Remember him?"

"Yes, and that's a good break," said Roger, with obvious satisfaction. "He'll have the thing sewn up before I get there."

"Want it easy, do you? Here's the play," Knightley went on. "We've got to see justice done, none of this one law for the rich and one law for the poor kind of stuff, and we've got to lean over backwards to make sure that the director isn't whitewashed. No one told me, and no one's telling you, but there's a possibility of a lot of trouble if this is badly handled, especially if it's something to do with a strike."

"You said—"

"Just check me when you get there," said Knightley. "What sergeant will you take?" "Sheppard, if he's free."

"I'll see that he's free," promised Knightley, and picked up a telephone. "It'll take you about half an hour to get out there. I've arranged for you to meet Old Charley at the Post Office in Elling at a quarter to five, he'll take you out to the factory and brief you on everybody in the case. Don't forget we could use quick results."

"If it was manslaughter—"

"We want the chap charged quick," Knightley said. "If it wasn't, we want all the answers that we're going to need for the Press, Parliament, and Transport House. Don't blame me, I didn't make society, I'm just a copper."

When Roger stood up, Knightley grinned, and added: "Forget my blather, Handsome. Willing to take a tip from me?"

"Glad to." Roger waited by the door.

"Don't put a foot wrong on this job. Even if it gets difficult, make quite sure of everything you do. Sir Ian Munro knows a lot of people who matter, and if you upset him they might not like it if you were promoted. We wouldn't like that to happen, would we?"

Roger said softly: "What's this, Joe?"

"Keep your nose clean for another ten days, and you'll have a desk and an office of your own," Knightley said. "That's not official, but you can kick me if I'm wrong."

"Joe," said Roger, his heart pounding, "if you're right, I stand you the best dinner you've had for years. You and your wife. I'll be seeing you."

So it was a journey to dreams.

Sheppard was a youngster, only twenty-seven, and fresh from a Division, where he had been recommended for the Yard. He had a pink face, childish even for his years, and when he took his hat off he made most people gasp: for he was nearly bald, with just a little hair down on his round, mushroom-shaped head. This baldness was the only thing he was self-conscious about, and he kept his hat on whenever he could. He had one of the most retentive memories of any man at the Yard, and therein lay his greatest value.

They reached the Post Office at one end of the wide, newly-built Elling High Street, at ten minutes to five. Old Charley Coombs wasn't in sight, but the car had hardly stopped before he came towards them from a doorway, a big burly man in a raincoat and, unexpectedly, a brand-new brown trilby. He was slightly splay-footed, making his movements seem slow and deliberate. Sheppard jumped out and opened the door, and Coombs heaved himself in.

"And don't tell me I'm not getting any thinner," he said. "My wife tells me that twice a day."

"I don't mind how much weight you've put on, provided you haven't got fatty degeneration of the brain tissues," Roger said. "Sergeant, this is the fabulous Charley Coombs, there's never been a man to touch him on fingerprints. Charley, this is Sergeant Sheppard."

"*Very* proud to meet you, sir," Sheppard said.

"If you take any notice of Handsome West's blarney, you won't go far at the Yard," said Coombs.

"Compliments over, what's it all about?" Roger asked.

"Turn right at the roundabout and then straight on for half a mile," said Coombs, easing himself up so as to loosen his raincoat. "I can tell you in a dozen sentences. The management and hands at Munro's have been spoiling for a fight for years. Robert Amory, the managing director, has got his head screwed on properly, and has pushed it off. The firm's just perfected the Munro Mark 9, which looks like taking the cream off the export market, and the labour leaders at the plant have seen their chance to get the biggest rise they've had for years. Sir Ian Munro, one of the old school sees himself more as a feudal baron than chairman of directors of a modern factory. Until about a year ago, his brother was chairman, and he was always on Amory's side. Now that Sir Ian is OC by seniority and shareholding, relations with the workers haven't been so good. Sir Ian's son, Malcolm, came into the firm and on to the Board recently. Rumour says that he didn't want to, but finally acceded to his father's wish. Army, travel, the type who'd prefer to be in a trans-Tibet expedition in a jeep or on a camel than at a desk. That's the general set-up."

"Thanks. When do I turn off?" Roger asked.

"Second right, then sharp left, and the factory will be straight in front of you, you can see the Powerhouse chimneys now. The trouble today started when the chief shop steward – the arch villain, according to Sir Ian – called a lunchtime meeting of the men and got a crowd of five or six hundred who were with him all the way: ten per cent rise or strike. You could almost see Sir Ian's gills flapping. Then young Malcolm comes up flaunting his Rolls-Bentley. Not exactly perfect timing." Charley Coombs grinned. "A youth started throwing oranges, and hit the car. Malcolm lost his temper and went after him, to give him the sack. The youth had friends, among them the brother of Michael Grannett, the chief shop steward. I haven't got the whole story yet, and I'm not sure who started the fight, but Malcolm taught the workers that you might run a Rolls-Bentley and wear Savile Row clothes, but it doesn't mean you can't use your fists."

"It's not easy to kill with fists," said Roger mildly.

"Don't know what killed young Roy Grannett, yet. He went down and hit his head an almighty crack on the ground, could have been that. He might have a thin skull, or what's-it-called, sub-something."

"Sub-arachnoid," Roger said, straightfaced.

"Too clever, that's your trouble. Anyway, he was helped to the factory hospital, and a nurse cleaned and bandaged his head, but didn't realise how badly hurt he was. He got weaker, a doctor saw him, and had him taken to hospital right away. He died under the anaesthetic"

"First thing we have to know for certain is the cause of death," Roger said, and turned where he had been told, then took a sharp left. This led him on to a long, wide road, with crisscross wire fencing on either side, and beyond the fences, hundreds upon hundreds of what looked like derelict cars, standing in rows. One huge mass of these stretched nearly out of sight. Not far off, a railway engine was puffing, and they could see cars being loaded on to wagons. The factory buildings were all one storey, and spread over a vast area. Two squat modern chimney stacks were giving off pale smoke. Half a dozen large lorries were being unloaded at a platform near the railway siding, where fifty or sixty men were in sight. Half a mile ahead was a gateway, open, with a gatehouse close to it.

Roger slowed down.

"Had time to judge the mood of the workers?" Roger inquired.

"Not really," Coombs answered. "The few I've spoken to since it got around that young Grannett was dead are more shocked than anything else. One or two breathed vengeance, of course, but one or two argued that if a chap could be killed in a fight like that, it might have happened any time."

"Usual mixture of common sense and irresponsibility," Roger mused prosily. "What was the mood before they knew he'd died?"

"That's easy. Like a lot of excited kids. I should think the factory lost an hour's production, there was so much talk about it." Coombs chuckled. "All the girls in the Assembly Shop, stores, and packing are on Malcolm's side, he's a handsome young buck. More Irish than Scottish in temper, too, like the whole family. The middle-aged and steadier chaps thought that young Grannett and the boy who threw the oranges were at least as much to blame as Malcolm. Bit scared, the steadier chaps, because they can see how this could be used to make real trouble. There's a lot of wild talk about Malcolm being the aggressor, and making him apologise, and a lot of resentment because he made Woods get his cards."

"Woods?"

"The orange-thrower. If I feel sorry for anyone in this, it's Woods," Coombs said. "He was egged on by young Grannett, not much doubt about that, and wishes he hadn't seen or smelt an orange in his life. He'll take it hard when he knows what happened."

"How will Malcolm Munro take it?"

"Funny thing, but he hasn't favoured me with his confidences. Tell you what, though."

"What?"

"He's sweet on his secretary, who used to be his Uncle Paul's secretary. Shows he has judgment, she's some girl. Properly handled, you might get more out of her than anyone else. Tell her you need all the information you can, get to help Malcolm, that kind of talk. Get young Sheppard to have a talk to her, too, he might be more effective, she'll probably feel that a sergeant is safer than a big shot."

They were slowing down as they neared the gates. A uniformed gatekeeper came out, dressed in a tailored blue raincoat and a blue peaked cap, then drew back as he saw Coombs.

"All right, sir, thank you."

Coombs nodded.

"Anything else you want to know before you start meeting people?" he demanded of Roger. "I'll do anything short of work miracles."

"What about this chief shop steward, Michael Grannett?" Roger asked. "What line is he likely to take?"

"I think you'll find that he'll be outwardly all sweet reason, but inwardly he may be fuming and hating. It's a funny thing with Grannett. I've often had a pint with him, and talked to other chaps who know him well. He's a decent-living, mild enough chap at home. Married, two children, pretty wife. But he's always needling the Munro management, and has always waged war with it. It's like a kind of vendetta," Coombs went on, and he was not a man given to flights of fancy. "But he's clever. On the works labour-force side there isn't anyone to touch him. On the managerial side he'd rise to the top. He knows the Factory Acts inside out, and never steps over the line, but he gets every penny and every concession he can for the workers generally."

"Sounds the kind of chap I'd like for my chief shop steward," Roger said. "In politics?"

"He's not a Commy, if that's what you mean. He's a member of the Labour Party, but not an active worker. Seems to think that he's destined to serve the workers at Munro's. The key to Michael Grannett, as far as I can see, is that he regards himself as dedicated, and thinks Sir Ian can do no right I'd say those two hate each other," Coombs went on. "But you aren't likely to catch Grannett doing anything he shouldn't."

Roger said: "Well, thanks for the picture, Charley, it's saved me hours of questioning, and I wouldn't have got it so clearly, anyhow. What did you want me to stop here for?"

"That's where it happened," Coombs said. "Those wooden boxes surround the spot where young Grannett fell, and the two in the middle cover bloodstains. There are some old bricks buried just beneath the surface, looks as though he fell on one. Thought I'd better fool you into thinking I knew something about the job! The Divisional chaps have already taken photographs, but I left everything untouched for you."

"Fine," said Roger. "Thanks."

"Who are you going to see first?" Coombs asked. "Workers or management?"

"Workers," said Roger promptly. "If I see the management first, some of the workers might get an idea that I'm on the management's side. What I'd like is to go straight to the Works Manager's office, and have a couple of witnesses to the fight meet me there. The directors can wait."

"You'll make an enemy of Sir Ian," Coombs said with a grin, "but that won't do you any harm. Colonel Harrison, the Works Manager, is on his side, anyhow. I take it you really want to see Michael Grannett first?"

"If he's available," Roger said, and stopped the car outside the building where Coombs told him to. "And then I want to see the hospital Sister, nurses, and anyone who was near Roy Grannett while he was in the First Aid quarters."

"Shouldn't be too difficult," Coombs said, "although there are three ways of getting to the place. I'll get it started."

The police car was opposite the office block, and Malcolm stood at his window, watching, while Tessa watched from hers. The fact that Coombs got out of the car probably meant that the Scotland Yard officials had arrived.

Tessa felt an almost irresistible desire to go and see Malcolm, but fought it back.

He had hardly spoken since the announcement of the youth's death. His father, although obviously badly shaken, had tried gruffly to reassure him. A. C. Cobb had seemed to shrink farther within his big white collar. Only Robert Amory had been able to help at all, by saying quietly: "We'll be firmly behind you, Malcolm, and you'll find that most of the people in the works will know that this death was accidental." Then he had paused, looked at the red-faced, hard-eyed, implacable, rather bitter man in the chair, and said very quietly: "We can't make any decision immediately, Ian. We ought to tell the workers' committee that we want at least twenty-four hours' grace. I'll get forty-eight hours, if I can. Do you agree?"

Sir Ian had given an imperceptible nod.

Malcolm had said: "Thanks, Bob," and gone to his own office. He hadn't moved from there since, and Tessa hadn't seen him.

Then, the handle of the door from his office turned and she swung round. She didn't know what to expect, but wasn't really surprised to see that he was outwardly unmoved, although the set of his lips and jaw seemed tighter, and his eyes might have been the eyes of a much older man.

"Find out where those Yard men are, will you? I want to go and see them," he said. He didn't smile.

Chapter Four

Sweet Reason

Coombs explained the layout of the factory buildings to Roger and Sheppard quickly and graphically. There were four main workshops, each vast in size, and the largest of them the Assembly Shop, where all the parts of the cars were brought for the final assembling. One of the other shops dealt exclusively with the bodies, including upholstery, another with the chassis, a third with the engines – and these were the three main component parts, which met and were put together in the Assembly Shop.

There were many smaller shops – the Paint Shop, the most modern of its kind in spite of the old-fashioned name, stores, Machine Shop for small tools, research, everything one would expect to find.

The Works Manager's office was in the Assembly Shop. Each of the other shops had its own manager, foremen, and shop stewards. Assembly was placed virtually in the centre of the plant, so that it was truly the hub of Munro Motors.

Roger sent Sheppard off to check with the Sister and nurses, then went into a large entrance hall, past the racks of cards by the six time-stamp clocks on either side, then through double doors into a mammoth shed which, at first sight, seemed all iron girders and masses of cars. It startled him. It took him several minutes to walk from the door to the offices, in the middle, with the big sign *Works Manager* above them, visible from any part of the shop. There were four rows of moving cars at the end where Roger was, and as he neared the offices, he saw how the different major component parts were assembled on a conveyor-belt system. At least three hundred men and half as many girls were in sight, all wearing khaki overalls. The clatter and rattle of the revolving conveyors, the hum of machinery, all the noises inseparable from a large factory, seemed to merge together in a tuneless cacophony. It was almost impossible to hear what Coombs was saying as he pointed out various things.

Coombs stopped, pointing.

"See that chap just going into the office?"

"The red-haired one?"

"Yes. That's Mike Grannett."

"Just as we wanted it," said Roger. "What did you say the manager's name was?"

"Colonel George Harrison. But I wouldn't be surprised if Amory was here, he's the real factory manager," Coombs explained. "Harrison is Sir Ian's brother-in-law. He'd never hold the job otherwise."

As they passed the men and girls, all performing some operation on the cars which slowly passed them by, or else stopped automatically, giving them time to finish the job they had to do, most people paused to look at Roger and his party. It was almost possible to hear them thinking: *The men from the Yard.* A short man in the now familiar khaki stood at a corner. Roger looked at him again, then grinned.

"Didn't know this was a home for old lags," he said to Coombs.

"You saw Pixie Parsons, did you?" Coombs had to raise his voice, but it carried only as far as Roger. "There are about a dozen of the Old Borstal Boys Association here. Haven't had any trouble with them yet. Don't get anything wrong, Handsome, Munro's aren't heartless. It's just that some of them are a bit old-fashioned." They reached the office.

This was a much larger building than it had seemed at first sight, built square, and with glass walls, so that the outer office staff could both see out and be seen. Inside were some offices with frosted glass, presumably all managerial. Raised higher than any of these was a kind of observation tower.

"That's the control room," Coombs said, "a sort of all-seeing eye. If anything goes wrong, everything can be stopped at the touch of a button. They've modernised everything."

He led the way into the offices, and along a glass-walled passage to the inner office, marked general. He opened the door without tapping, and went in.

Roger followed closely.

Michael Grannett was sitting on the corner of a desk, where a girl in a black dress sat typing. He looked round. Roger's first impression was of an earnest, good-looking man; for some reason he was surprised that Grannett wore rimless glasses – not pince-nez, but with gold-coloured arms and thick hooked ends to go over the ears. His hair seemed more auburn than red in this fluorescent light. He had a good, square chin, and curiosity seemed to show in his expression.

Coombs said: "Hallo, Mike. I can't tell you how sorry I am."

Grannett said: "Thanks, Charley."

"Like you to meet Chief Inspector West of New Scotland Yard, an old friend of mine," said Coombs.

Grannett stood up, and Roger shook hands. Full face, Grannett looked nearer forty than thirty, and his thick hair was receding from his temples. He had grey-green eyes, and they didn't smile, although his lips did. He looked shocked; almost dazed.

"Glad to know you, Chief Inspector."

"I wish we could help," Roger said.

He was startled by the change in Grannett's expression, by the glint which drove the shadows out of the man's eyes for a moment, and by the strength of his fingers as he gripped his arm.

"You can help," Grannett declared, in a thin voice. "You can see that Munro isn't allowed to get away with this. It was cold-blooded murder."

"Now, Mike—" Coombs began.

"Oh, you have to be on the side of the management, you know which side your bread is buttered," Grannett said, "but I tell you it was murder. Roy was just a kid. He didn't stand a chance. Munro was two stone heavier and as good as a professional. He meant to teach Roy and everyone with him a lesson, he meant to show them who was boss. Don't make any mistake about that. It wasn't just a slap down, he meant to do Roy injury." His eyes were narrowed and glittering still, and he uttered the words through lips which hardly seemed to move. His fists were clenched tightly by his sides, and obviously it would not take much to make him lose his self-control completely.

He rasped: "Well, Chief Inspector, isn't that murder?"

"That's not for me to say," Roger said. "It—"

"It's for you to say all right. Listen to me, Mr West – and you, Charley. As sure as I'm standing here, if Munro isn't arrested and charged with his crime, if he isn't punished just as severely as the law can punish him, I'll punish him myself. He's not going to get away with

"Mike, take it easy," Coombs urged.

Grannett didn't say anything else. It was hard to be sure whether he meant exactly what he said; whether this was really the consequences of pent-up bitterness, or whether it had been born out of the shock of his brother's death.

"In your position I think I'd feel the same," Roger said quietly, "even if I'd know it was crazy to say it. I'll see that the law is properly carried out, Mr Grannett."

"That's all I ask," Grannett said, and dropped on to the corner of the desk again, took a handkerchief out of his pocket, and dabbed at his forehead. He had gone very red, and the navy-blue suit he was wearing threw up the flood of colour vividly. Roger saw that his big, strong hands were well kept, and that the suit was well pressed and brushed; his shoes were highly polished.

He said: "I've just come back from the hospital, and I saw Roy on a slab. So don't think I don't mean what I say." He took out cigarettes, and then unexpectedly burst out: "Goddam the no-smoking rule!"

"Break it for once," Coombs said, "no one here is going to work to rule on this."

He broke off as another door opened, and two men appeared, one short, grey-haired, stocky, the other tall and round-faced. Before they came into the room, Coombs whispered into Roger's ear: "Tall one's Robert Amory, the other's Colonel Harrison."

He straightened up, much as he would have done in the old days when the Assistant Commissioner appeared.

"Good afternoon, sir."

Amory said: "Hallo, Coombs, I won't keep you a moment." His clear, calm blue eyes seemed to absorb all there was to see of Roger and Coombs, and then he looked at Grannett, giving him his full attention. "Ah, Grannett. I won't waste words, but I must say that I am terribly grieved and shocked. I speak for everyone when I say that we only want to make what amends we can."

Would Grannett flare up again?

He didn't; he didn't speak at all.

"I asked to see you, if you came back; your deputy, if you didn't," Amory went on. "Do you feel up to talking business?"

Grannett said, "Yes," in a hard voice.

"Then if you'll come into Colonel Harrison's office – I'm sure these gentlemen will excuse us for a few minutes – we can talk."

"All you have to say is yes or no, isn't it?" asked Grannett, in the same hard voice. "We've made our claim. You undertook to give us the answer by five o'clock this afternoon. It's ten-past five now."

"True enough," said Amory. "And you won't want me to bandy words, Grannett. So I'll be quite frank with you. It seems to the Board that to try to reach a considered decision in view of what has just happened would be unwise. I—no, let me finish, please. It is now Wednesday. We would like two more days to consider the issues, and I hope that on behalf of the workers you will agree to it. A forced decision is never a good one, and the present circumstances could hardly be less auspicious."

Roger studied each man, and couldn't even begin to anticipate how Grannett would respond, although he had already come to respect the chief shop steward for unexpected qualities. Now Grannett stood silent, eyeing the managing director; it seemed obvious that the Works Manager was of little account. But there was a kind of strength in him; Roger had a feeling that he was holding himself in with an effort. Harrison, too; Harrison wasn't a man to write off, and there was a peculiar brilliance in his eyes.

The silence seemed to last for a long time.

Then Grannett took a cigarette from the packet he had been holding in his hand all the time, and put it to his lips. A few minutes ago he had hesitated to do this, because observance of the factory rule was so drilled into him; so this was defiance, or genuine forgetfulness. He lit the cigarette from a lighter. He put both lighter and packet away. He blew out of the side of his mouth, and then answered in a high-pitched voice.

"That's fair enough. I'm not in a mood to be dispassionate, either. Friday, five o'clock, and there won't be any more delays?"

"There will not."

"Then I'll recommend the employees to accept the postponement."

"Thank you, Grannett," Amory said quietly, "I'm sure you're wise."

Grannett said: "I hope so. Good night," and turned sharply on his heel. Years of Army square bashing were in that movement and in the sharp click of his heels.

"If there is anything at all we can do to help—"

Amory began.

Grannett stopped at the other door, and said icily: "You could give my mother back her younger son, and me back a brother. That's all we want." He looked away from Amory to Roger, and added in a way that was almost a sneer: "By five o'clock on Friday perhaps you'll have finished your job, too."

He went out.

"I'm sorry that we had such a delay, Chief Inspector," Amory said two minutes afterwards, when they were in Harrison's office, with Harrison standing silently watching all of them with those unnaturally brilliant grey eyes. "I don't know anything about official inquiries such as this, but I can assure you that everything you require will be put at your disposal. I imagine you will want somewhere to work from, and an office either here or in the main office building will be made available. Mr Coombs will be at your service. You may have free access to all parts of the factory, and absolute freedom to question any individual, either among the workers, the office staff, the management, or for that matter the Board. We want to assist in every way possible, Mr West, you have only to ask for what you want."

He was half a head taller than Roger, he spoke quietly and impressively, and it was obvious that he meant what he said. Now and again Harrison gave a brisk nod, as if anxious to assert himself.

"Thank you, sir," Roger said formally. "I'd like to see three or four witnesses of the incident first, one at a time, and preferably persons not related to or closely associated with the dead youth. Then I'll have a word with my sergeant, who is checking with the First Aid people. After that, I'd like to see Mr Malcolm Munro."

"Coombs told me you would certainly want to see some witnesses, and I have six who have agreed to stay late – the afternoon shift finished at five-thirty, you understand."

"They'll be paid overtime rates, of course," Harrison put in, with the air of a man making a statement of high policy.

"Where would you like to have your office, Chief Inspector?" Amory asked.

"Here, sir, please," Roger smiled.

"Good. Colonel Harrison will show you where it is, and unless there is anything else you want me for, I'd like to go over to the office building."

When Roger said: "You're quite free to go, sir," Amory hesitated, and then added very quietly: "Thank you. I would like you to know this, Chief Inspector. Everyone is greatly distressed about this unfortunate accident, none more so than my fellow director, Mr Malcolm Munro."

"I'm sure," Roger said formally.

Amory went off, bending his head a little because the doors were on the low side. Harrison now came into his own, and talked bluffly, rather like a recording of everything Amory had said, as he led the way into a small office, with a large desk, three telephones, blotting-paper, a writing-pad, pen and ink, and standing by the side, a dictaphone. The walls were of frosted glass, and there was a door which presumably led to the outside passage and the factory itself.

"This will be at your disposal," Harrison declared. "Call on me for everything you want, please. May I express the hope that your investigations into the accident will not be unduly prolonged?"

"It won't take a minute longer than I can help, sir."

Harrison nodded, and went out. Coombs closed the door firmly behind him, but as the latch clicked a man came up and opened the door. It was Sheppard.

"Come in," Roger said. "How have you been doing?"

"The First Aid Rooms can all be approached from three different ways, to make 'em easy to access," Sheppard reported. "The Sister is worked up because she didn't realise how badly the boy was hurt."

"What makes her so worked up?"

"Injured pride, I'd say," said Sheppard. "I came straight back because she's the only day-duty First Aid person still there. Don't know if you agree, sir, but it doesn't seem worth going out after the others tonight. They'll all be on duty by eight o'clock in the morning."

"We'll let 'em wait," Roger agreed, and turned to Coombs. "Call that Sister on the blower and tell her I'd like a word before she goes."

Coombs nodded, picked up the receiver, and asked for the Sister. Sheppard looked puzzled, but Roger didn't explain until Coombs said into the telephone: "Okay," and then rang off. "She's been gone five minutes. Think it's worth calling her back? "

"Might as well wait for the autopsy report, we don't want to start a hare," Roger said.

"I may be dim-witted, but what are you two getting at?" Sheppard asked.

Roger motioned to Coombs.

"Tell him, Charley."

"Look at it this way, Sheppy," the ex-Yard man said. "A boy who's pretty tough and eager for a fight bangs his head on the ground. Perhaps he hit a buried brick, perhaps he didn't. Damned bad luck a fall like that should kill him – bad for him, bad for Malcolm Munro, in a lesser degree. Handsome and I asked ourselves if it's as simple as it looks. Then the Sister starts saying she didn't realise how badly the boy was hurt. You don't get a job like hers at a place like Munro's unless you're good. Judging the seriousness or otherwise of a head injury should be easy – at least, as far as saying whether it's superficial or not. This Sister plumped for the injuries being superficial – but he died from them. Now she 'can't believe' she made a mistake." Coombs paused, as if for breath, and then challenged: "See?"

"You mean, could the injuries have become worse after she'd examined Roy Grannett?" Sheppard asked slowly.

"You're on the ball," Coombs approved. "Yes, that's it, eh, Handsome?"

"That's it – and if they became worse, how did they?" Roger said. "Did he fall off the couch? Bang his head against a wall, or—"

"Did someone hit him!" cried Sheppard. "My God, that would be—"

"Don't even mention the word," Coombs warned.

"Certainly not until we've seen the medical and the pathologist's reports," Roger said. "There's your next angle, Sheppy. Get hold of another telephone, call the hospital, and go and see them if necessary. Talk to the works' doctor and everyone who saw young Grannett when he was in the sick-bay or whatever they call it. Charley will help fix all that, won't you, Charley?"

"Nice to see you're making a job of it. Yes, I'll fix it all." Coombs had the light of excitement in his eyes. "You might have told Harrison you wanted two offices, and not left it to me."

"Just blame the Yard," Roger said briskly. "Then lay on these witnesses of the fight, will you?"

Sheppard went off, obviously excited, and Roger switched to the six witnesses who had stayed late. Each story was substantially the same. Two youngish men were evidently bitterly resentful towards Malcolm Munro. Two elderly men tried to make it clear that they thought the director had acted under severe provocation. Two were neutral. Under questioning, each of them admitted that Munro had gone for Grannett furiously, and that the youth hadn't had a chance.

All agreed that when he had fallen, Munro had stood back; there was no question of an attack while he had been on the ground. No one seemed to think that Munro and Roy Grannett had known each other before, and there seemed no reason to believe that there was any personal motive behind the savagery with which Munro had gone into the attack.

The younger witnesses said that Munro had started the fight.

The others said that he had been pushed from behind, bumping into Grannett, who had promptly struck out.

Roger asked each man in turn: "Did you think Roy Grannett was badly hurt?"

And the answer was "No," in each case.

"Did he seem to hit the ground hard enough to injure him badly?"

"No."

"Were you surprised to hear that he was dead?"

"Yes."

The Sister had been, too, and her professional pride had been stung. Roger was anxious to get the medical report, almost as anxious to see Munro and size up the young director for himself, but wasn't sure whether it would be better to bring Munro here or to go to the director's office in the main building.

There were undercurrents which could sweep him right off course if he were not very careful; tensions which could become explosive. It was an atmosphere he'd heard about but never experienced, worker-employer relationship at breaking point.

If he showed the slightest sign of leaning one way or the other, he could easily make things worse. Emotionally, the workers were probably more sensitive, but if he veered too much in their favour, it might have a chilling effect on the management, and lose him their co-operation.

He had to look as if he was sitting on the fence. The best way would be to be ultra-polite when alone with the management, deferring in manner if not in fact: but be more bluff with the workers, giving an impression that at heart he was one of them.

He decided to see Malcolm there, and telephoned the director's office. A girl answered.

"This is Mr Malcolm's secretary."

It was half past six, and that meant that the girl, Tessa Lee, was working late. Was it true that Munro was 'sweet' on her? If so, did she feel the same way about Munro? Had Coombs meant that there was a genuine love affair, or had he implied that the association was man and mistress? In a different kind of investigation, Roger would need to find out at once; but he didn't see that it mattered yet.

"Is Mr Malcolm Munro there, please?"

"Who shall I say wants him?"

"Chief Inspector West, speaking from the Works Office."

"Oh, yes," the girl said. She wasn't flurried or flustered and had a nice speaking voice. "I'll put you through." There was only a momentary pause, before a man said: "Mr West? Would you like to see me?"

"Yes, please, if it's convenient for you to come here."

"I'll be right over," Munro promised, and rang off.

There was nothing in his voice or manner to suggest that he was on edge, but one of the advantages of a good education, and of military added to public-school training, was that it was easy to hide one's feelings. Did this Munro feel guilty as hell, or was he indifferent? Had Mike Grannett been right when he had said that Munro had set out to teach the men a lesson, had meant to establish who was boss? Or had that idea been born out of Grannett's deep sense of dedication to the cause of the workers?

A telephone bell rang. Roger hadn't yet discovered which bell was attached to which instrument, made a wrong guess, then picked up the right one. It was Sheppard.

"I'm at the Elling Hospital, sir. I've just been talking to Mr Cartwright, the surgeon who performed the operation on Roy Grannett. I think you ought to come and see him as soon as you can."

"Why?" demanded Roger.

"There are one or two factors which seem a bit peculiar, sir," Sheppard told him, and then added cautiously: "Unusual, sir, perhaps I should say."

The Sister's attitude began to look much more significant.

"How long will Mr Cartwright be at the hospital?" Roger asked.

"Until half past seven, he ... just a moment, sir ..." There was a pause. Then: "He says that if you can't get here by then, he'll be glad to see you at his home any time after nine o'clock. I'll get the address."

"Right. Thank him for me," said Roger, and rang off.

Sheppard had said just enough, but been cautious over the telephone. He was as good as sergeants came, Roger decided, and he made some notes, guessing that it would be five minutes or more before young Munro arrived.

Tessa felt Malcolm's fingers firm on her shoulder when he left the office, but he didn't say a word. He had said very little since the Board meeting, and she wasn't at all sure what he was thinking; she suspected that he was going through a kind of private hell. It was hopeless to try to help; nothing could alter the fact that the youth had been killed as a result of the fight.

What could anyone feel, having caused a human being's death?

Tessa turned to the window and looked into the window-lit grounds. The night shift had been at work for over an hour, every light in the factory seemed to be on, except those in this general office building. Floodlights blazed upon the loading and unloading platforms. The tragedy of the labour crisis was in its timing. They were working two shifts and sometimes three, after several years of short time or limited shifts. They had been difficult years, but Mark 9 had lifted them right out of the troubles. If there were a long strike ...

The telephone bell rang, and Tessa turned round and picked it up without rounding the desk, which was quite empty. There was nothing to keep her here, and Malcolm had told her to go home, just before he had squeezed her shoulder and left.

Probably only he knew that she was still here.

Her heart began to beat very quickly.

"Tessa, I thought you were still here, you always tell me when you're going." It was the operator on duty, Moira Sharp. "I say, I wouldn't breathe a word to anyone else, but I've just got to tell someone or I'll scream I There's something funny about Roy Grannett's death."

Tessa's heart seemed to stop.

"What on earth do you mean?"

"Well, I only heard by accident. I was putting a call through to that Chief Inspector West—isn't he a looker, by the way? I didn't think that policemen were like that – and I happened to hear a sentence or two. The Scotland Yard sergeant was talking to West, and he asked West to go and see the surgeon who started the operation. Apparently there's something 'peculiar', that's the very word he used. What do you think it could be?"

Tessa made herself say: "I haven't the faintest idea, and for goodness' sake don't go spreading this around."

"Oh, I won't, you can count on me! But I just had to unburden myself to someone. How *is* he, dear?"

"Who?"

"Now, Tess! Your Malcolm."

"Moira, you really mustn't talk like that, it just isn't justified," Tessa said, and felt helpless to a point of uselessness. "I don't know much more than you do. He hasn't said a word since he heard what had happened, and there's no reason why he should talk to me. Moira, I hope you'll make quite sure that you won't—"

There was a shout from outside, then a scuffling, all sounding very clear through the open window. There came more shouting and scuffling, followed by a sharp explosive sound, like a fire cracker. Tessa leaned forward quickly, to look out of the window, leaving the other girl hanging on, and she saw a dozen or more shadowy figures, all men, surrounding one man who stood alone about thirty yards away from the steps of the office entrance.

The lone man was Malcolm.

The others were attacking him, and some of them had sticks.

Chapter Five

Cry Vengeance

As he stepped from the hallway of the office building, Malcolm Munro shivered. It was much colder than it had been during the early afternoon, and wind was sweeping across wasteland beyond the factory. There were odd little sounds, as of paper and leaves frisking along the ground, and rustling in the shrubs and the trees which grew outside the building He saw two or three men some distance off, clear in the light of one of the workshop buildings; no one seemed near.

He noticed that the night commissionaire wasn't on duty; that needed putting right. It was Harrison's job, and what little he knew of the Works Manager suggested that it would not be done until he was told. Harrison was an odd fish, ex-cavalry, Sir Ian's brother-in-law, loyal, wholly reliable, and completely unimaginative.

Malcolm wondered what the Yard man would be like.

He glanced up at the window of Tessa's office, hoping that she would be standing there; if she was, he would wave, and if he waved and anyone saw him, gossip would spread all over the works by tomorrow. So he wouldn't wave. He saw the back of her head, and fancied that she was at the telephone.

He turned away from her.

For the first time, he realised that several men were in the shadows at the far end of the building, all moving towards him. There was nothing sinister about this, as far as he could see, it was simply puzzling; the kind of thing that happened during the lunch hour, or other mealtime breaks. Many of the workers liked to sit and look over the lawns at the far end of the office building, which were floodlit by night. But this wasn't a mealtime.

Running footsteps sounded behind him, and he looked round. Three or four men were rushing at him from the far end of the building.

Then he realised what this was all about.

The light was good enough to show that three men, coming fast, were between him and the factory buildings. Two others were between him and the entrance to the office block, cutting him off from that; and at least four were approaching from each end of the building. Three or four were carrying long sticks.

Then something smacked heavily into the ground at his feet, and something else whizzed over his head.

He could run.

If he did, there would be a reasonable chance of dodging the men between him and the factory workshops, and reaching sanctuary there; he was quick on his feet and quicker off the mark than most. But if he ran it would show that he was frightened. Things were already bad enough; but if the word 'coward' was flung at him he might as well throw his hand in.

He had only seconds in which to make up his mind.

A stone caught him on the shoulder.

He spoke sharply, voice clear on the wind. "What the devil do you think you're doing? Get back to work."

"We'll show you what we're doing," one of the nearer men growled, "we're going to make you wish you'd never been born."

A stone struck Malcolm on the arm.

One man was nearer than the rest, big, youngish, his face set and grim; he didn't carry a stick. Tackle him, beat him, and it might win time, might keep Malcolm on his feet until help came.

Help?

He leaped at the man.

They met, body to body. As they collided, Malcolm knew that this wouldn't be easy and might not even be possible; there was hard, brutish strength in the other. Of course there was: they would choose someone powerful, someone able to do to him what he had done to young Grannett. He took a slug of a blow on his chin, and it hurt. He got through the other's guard with a hook and a straight left, then felt himself seized and held in a hug with arms so powerful that he felt as if his ribs would crack. One moment he had been breathing normally; the next the breath seemed to be squeezed out of his body, and he couldn't draw another in. It was like being suffocated.

It was like being crushed.

But he had been trained to kill, and all his military training came to his aid. He brought his right knee up viciously, felt the brute sag, heard him grunt. He freed himself from those bear-like arms, rammed both fists savagely into the man's stomach, and won the satisfaction of seeing him staggering away. But that was only one man out of a dozen. He felt a sharp blow at the side of his head which hadn't been caused by a fist, but a stick. He saw a man making another sweeping blow at him, and shot out his hand. In a lucky snatch his fingers closed round the weapon, which was smooth like a broomstick. He wrenched it free and swept it round, catching the man on the crown of the head, so two were momentarily out of action.

Another stick jabbed him in the ribs; yet another cracked on his legs; a stone caught him in the nape of the neck. All he could do was to swing the broomstick round and round, hoping to keep the gang at bay; but he knew that he hadn't a chance. A man darted behind him, thrust a stick between his legs, and levered it.

Malcolm crashed down.

He thought: "This is it," and covered his head in his hands. He felt their heavy, steel-tipped boots, the sticks, the murderous intent, and wondered how long he would suffer, how long he would be conscious.

And he wondered if they meant to kill.

It was the moment when Malcolm wrested the stick from one of his assailants that Tessa saw what was happening. She sprang round and cried into the telephone: "There's a gang, attacking Malcolm! Send help at once!"

"Wha—" Moira began.

Tessa dropped the receiver without noticing that it didn't fall squarely on its platform, and ran to the door, out into the wide, carpeted passage to the general office, across this and past three women cleaners, who gaped at her. They couldn't help. She didn't waste breath speaking to them, but reached the swing doors which led to the first-floor landing. No one was here, either. She raced down the stairs, with no more idea of what she could do than when she had left the office, knowing only that she must do something, those men might kill Malcolm. She reached the great marble hall, where the night commissionaire should be; but no one was on duty, the whole of the ground floor seemed to be deserted.

She reached the top of the steps.

In the dim light, for the floodlamps were out, she saw a dozen men in a struggling, seething heap, and knew that Malcolm wasn't in sight. So he must be underneath them.

She screamed for help as she ran down the steps, then caught her foot against a stone, and lost her balance. It took seconds to steady herself, and each one was agonising. Yet the pause brought relief. A shrill whistle sounded above all other noises, and immediately the seething mass of bodies seemed to rise up, as in an eruption. Men sprang away from the spot and turned and ran. Tessa did not know why and did not even think of a reason. They were running; and Malcolm lay on the ground, quite still.

She could not reach him quickly enough, but she was terribly afraid.

He did not move.

Other things moved. Engines were roaring, men shouted, car headlamps spread a wanted light, but Tessa was aware of none of these. She reached Malcolm, almost fell down on her knees beside him, and cried his name over and over again, quite distraught. He lay with his legs stretched out, one arm under, one arm over his head, as if he had tried to protect himself. Somehow, she fought panic back, and managed to turn him round enough to see his face.

There was a trickle of something dark at one lip. Blood. His eyes were closed.

She fought for self-control

"Malcolm, darling," she said hoarsely. "You'll be all right, darling, don't worry, you'll be all right." She heard footsteps nearby, and looked round, still holding Malcolm close. "Please get a doctor," she begged of a man who was just a creature on two legs, a dark head outlined against the white building.

"It's all right, Miss Lee, I've sent for one." This was Robert Amory, and he bent down on the other side of Malcolm. "There is no need to worry." How did he know, the fool? "Ease him round this way a little, will you?" he asked, and felt for Malcolm's pulse. The calm way he did that made Tessa feel ashamed of her own panic; and for the first time she realised just what she had done.

The director must have heard her saying so desperately: "Malcolm, darling."

She shivered, suddenly chilled, and stared into Amory's face as he held Malcolm's wrist, then saw him relax and smile. "Not much the matter there," he assured her, "nothing that a rest won't cure, anyhow. Ask one of the car drivers to turn the car this way so that we can have more light, will you? I'd like to have a look at his face."

She got up and did what he told her; and she shivered again. A dozen men were here now, and more were coming, and there were three cars, including Amory's. As she told a driver what to do, her teeth began to chatter.

"You'd better get inside, you need a drink," the driver said. "Hey! Charley! You there, Charley? Better come and look after Miss Lee, she's just about all in."

Roger glanced up from studying notes and reports while waiting for young Munro, realised that it was a quarter of an hour since he had telephoned him, and said aloud: "The fool can't have ducked out, can he?" when a telephone rang again. This time he was right at the first pick; and this time it was a stranger's voice, rather agitated.

"Is that Chief Inspector West?"

"Yes."

"I've a message from Mr Coombs, sir. He says that Mr Malcolm Munro was attacked in the grounds, and will you come to the office building at once?"

Roger said sharply: "Is he badly hurt?"

"I don't know anything more, sir."

"I'll be right over," Roger promised, and was on his feet before putting the receiver down. He took his hat from a hook behind the door and hurried out into the brightly lit passage.

It was odd to be there with windows overlooking the vast Assembly Shop; to see the fabulous conveyors making the cars look like giant caterpillars clinging to the spindly veins of moving leaves. He stepped into the shop itself, and had to pause to make sure which way to go. Then he moved at the double. Dozens of people stared, the night shift obviously knew as much as the day shift, but no one stopped him. The noise was still deafening, but he noticed some workmen talking to each other, and they did not appear to shout. He reached the main entrance, and saw the office block about two hundred yards away. The floodlights were on now, showing everything clearly. Silhouetted against the white building and against the headlamps of cars were a dozen or so men, and the big figure of Charley Coombs was unmistakable among them. Then Roger heard Sheppard call out from one side.

"That you, sir? ... Oh, yes." He came over at the double. "I've just got back. What's on?"

"Just going to find out," said Roger. "Stop running, we've got time. What did this surgeon say? Give me more detail, will you?"

"He said that there's a possibility that Grannett was killed *after* the scrap, sir. Says that there are injuries at the back of the head which aren't consistent with a heavy fall or with being punched. More like a kick or a blow. I didn't want to say too much over the telephone."

"You were quite right. What's the surgeon like?"

"Mr Cartwright, sir? He seems to know his onions."

"I've asked the hospital to let a Home Office pathologist have a look at the body," Roger said. "Did he know that?"

"Oh, yes, and I understand that Dr Legg's on the way already, they were preparing for him in the hospital laboratory. No doubt everyone's getting a move on."

"Too much of a move on, in some ways," Roger said, and chuckled. "Forget that! And thanks. Stand by until I tell you what to do. Coombs has already got cracking, I fancy. Now *we* can get a move on." He broke into a run, which brought them to the little group of men and the cars. Suddenly, lights in the office building were switched on, so that they could see everyone clearly – and there was Charley Coombs, on one knee, peering at something on the ground.

"Like to borrow a magnifying glass, Charley?" Roger asked.

Coombs grunted.

"So you don't sleep all the time."

"What's on?"

"They tried to murder Malcolm Munro, that's what's on."

"Badly hurt?" Roger's voice became sharp.

"Knocked out, and a cut and a bruise or two. That—er, his secretary happened to see it out of the window, and her screams brought help. The attack was pretty well planned," Coombs went on, standing up. "There were a dozen or so of the young brutes with scouts on either side. As soon as help was on the way, the scouts whistled and the attackers ran off. Didn't see one of them clearly."

"What've you done?" asked Roger.

"Sent for you, and found one or two broomsticks they dropped, you ought to get some dabs on them."

"Had the gates locked? The fence guarded?"

Coombs gulped. "Gawd, no, I forgot."

"Who's in charge here?" Roger asked, and looked round at the assembled Divisional policemen. No one answered. "Do a job for me, quick, will you?" he asked generally. "Two men go to the main gatehouse, and ask the gatekeeper to lock it and take the name of every man who wants to get through – hold anyone who insists, ask the others to wait. Two more go to the loading platforms and do the same thing. Then get permission to have a watch on the fence surrounding the factory. We want to try to catch some of the chaps who did it. All set?"

There was a moment's hesitation before a man said: "Come on, Bill."

"Like me at the gatehouse, sir?" Sheppard asked.

"Good idea. See if the gatekeeper can name everyone who's been out in the last twenty minutes or so. Get a list of them." Roger stopped and watched the men hurrying off, all glad to have something specific to do; then he became aware of the fact that Coombs was grinning.

"What's funny, Charley?"

"Did me good to hear you on the job," declared Coombs. "If you aren't Commander one of these days, I'll eat my hat. Anything you'd like me to do?"

"Yes. Phone the Division, then have this spot cordoned off and searched for anything the thugs might have dropped," Roger said crisply. "We'll want a thorough search all over the grounds, as soon as there's enough daylight. If they get away with an attack like this, they'll probably have another crack before we can turn round. What's this about the girl, Tessa Lee? See her yourself?"

"I happened to be coming up with Mr Amory, in his car," Coombs explained. "He'd been home for half an hour, he lives only a couple of miles away, and I'd been having a word with the gatekeeper. We were the first on the scene. I rounded some chaps up while Amory went to the girl and Malcolm M. I stayed long enough to hear the way she went on. She's so much in love with him, the thought that he might be hurt terrified her."

"Where is she now?"

"In the office First Aid Room. Each building's got First Aid quarters, and the hospital itself is at the back of this office block. Amory's gone with her and two or three others."

"Anyone see the attack?"

"Not at close quarters, as far as I can make out," Coombs said. "The night-duty commissionaire was having a cup of tea, instead of being on the job."

"Was he, then," remarked Roger. "Could he have been dropped a pound to turn a blind eye?"

"Wouldn't put it past him."

"We'll check," Roger said, and went on with hardly a pause: "Seen Mike Grannett lately?"

"No."

"Job to do there," said Roger, and looked towards the gatehouse, going on almost regretfully, "I shouldn't have let Sheppard go. I want to find out where Grannett's been, whether he was back in the grounds, whether he could have organised this job. You say there were a dozen men?"

"At least," Coombs asserted. "The Division will do all that's necessary with Grannett, Handsome. Why don't you call 'em from the office? "

"I will," said Roger.

He went towards the steps, where now a uniformed commissionaire stood in an attitude that was almost bellicose, and demanded to see his pass. Roger showed his card, and the man almost quivered in apology.

"Where's Miss Lee, do you know?

"In the First Aid Room, sir. Mr Amory's there with her, and Night Sister's come down from the hospital. I had to nip off duty for five minutes, sir, but if I'd known what was coming, I wouldn't have moved an inch."

"Too bad," Roger said. It wasn't his job to dress this man down, or to act as if he were to blame. Yet. "Where is the First Aid Room?"

"Through those doors and second on the left, sir."

"Thanks." Roger stood aside as the man rushed to open the swing doors which led to the main office entrance, and then turned left along a wide, brightly lit passage. The second door was painted white, with a large red cross on it, and the words first aid painted in black. He opened the door and went in, without knocking. There were two rooms, this outer or ante-room, where two nurses were standing, and a second one, the door of which was wide open and which seemed to be much larger.

"Excuse me, sir—" a nurse began.

Roger gave his most pleasant smile. "Police," he said, and went into the big room.

Chapter Six

Bad Mistake

The only one who noticed Roger was Amory, who glanced up, nodded, then looked back at the couch where Malcolm Munro lay with his eyes open. Another nurse, probably the Night Sister, was dabbing at his nose, which was badly grazed on one side; his lips were swollen, and so was his right ear, but his colour wasn't bad, and there was nothing to suggest that he was badly hurt.

By his side, standing up, was a girl whom Roger hadn't seen before.

The Lee girl, of course.

She had less colour than young Munro, and her eyes looked too bright; glassy, as if with pain or shock. Apart from that, she was really something to see, a brunette with wavy hair which clustered about a round head, framing a strikingly attractive face. One of the classic types. She wore a summer-weight grey coat, which hung open and showed her black skirt and white blouse. Some reddish brown smears on the blouse, close to the neck and the right breast, looked like blood: that would be where she had cradled Malcolm in her arms. Quite a girl; quite a figure. She was very much on edge, and once or twice glanced at Amory, who seemed intent only on what the Night Sister was doing. Then Malcolm Munro looked towards Roger, and his eyes asked the obvious question.

"This is Chief Inspector West," Amory said, "but I'm sure Mr West won't insist on questioning you tonight."

"Don't see why not." Munro spoke thickly, and only one side of his mouth moved; the other, swollen, was almost certainly cut on the inside, and must be very painful. "I'm all right, no need to fuss. Sorry I kept you waiting, Chief Inspector." Well, that showed spirit. "Finished with me, Sister?"

He wasn't exactly arrogant, but wasn't far from it. His eyes glinted as if he wanted to grin, and Roger's first feeling was one of admiration, for Munro must have had a hell of a time.

"You really must rest, Mr Munro." The Sister was anxious.

"You're very good," said Munro, "but I assure you that it's possible for a man to walk ten miles with a hole in his side big enough to take my fist, and have a chat with the C.O. at the end of it. What I would like is a drink. Lend me a hand, Tessa." He put his large, brown hand towards the Lee girl, and she took it eagerly, but shot a glance at Amory, who watched without any sign of approval or disapproval. "I assure you that if I feel like collapsing, Sister, I'll come back and admit that you were right," Munro added, and stood up.

He didn't sway. That probably cost quite an effort

"We'll go along to the waiting-room, I've arranged for everything we need to be there," Amory said. "Will you go ahead and make sure everything's all right, Miss Lee?"

"Yes, of course." The girl let Munro's hand go, and hurried towards the door; she moved well. Munro watched and, even when she had gone out of sight, looked as if he could still see her. Then he gave a twisted grin at Amory and said: "I think I'd better tackle one kind of trouble at a time, Bob. I take it that you wanted Tessa out of the way while the Chief Inspector puts me through the hoop."

"It seemed wise," said Amory dryly.

Roger said quietly: "What I want, Mr Munro, is a straightforward factual account of what happened from the time you reached the gatehouse in your car this afternoon. After that I may have one or two specific questions to ask."

There was a pause, while Munro watched Roger as if he was making up his mind what to say. To lie? He almost certainly realised his own danger: that if it could be proved that he had started the fight, he would be charged with manslaughter. As a director of Munro Motors, he would probably be finished for life.

"Straightforward and factual," he echoed at last. "All right. I was a damned fool, and—"

"Stop that, Malcolm." Amory's voice could be sharp and incisive. Munro flashed a glance at him.

"Oh, not an actionable fool. Just a straightforward red one. I ..."

He had an exceptional aptitude for summarising facts, and if Roger had to set down the story he had heard from several sources, it would be almost word for word with Munro's statement.

"Thank you," Roger said when it was done. "How well did you know Roy Grannett, Mr Munro?"

"I didn't know him at all."

"Hadn't you seen him about the works?"

"Possibly. I didn't recognise him, although I did recognise young Woods."

"Did you know Woods?"

"Yes, as an errand boy during the week or two I spent in the Assembly Shop. He was the chief tea-maker. I was not on terms of any kind of friendship with any of the youths, or any of the men in the factory. It might have been better if I had got to know some of them."

"Chief Inspector, I think I must insist that you stop questioning Mr Munro now," Amory intervened quietly. "He looks very pale, and undoubtedly is suffering from severe shock. I want to send him home to bed."

"Nothing more I need worry him or you about at the moment, sir," Roger said, and flashed his smile. Be reasonable, always be reasonable. "Thank you for being so helpful." He turned towards the door.

"May I ask what you're going to do next?" Amory asked.

Roger said: "Look for the bad men – the hooligans who attacked Mr Munro."

"I hope you don't lay hands on them," said Munro. "They've probably cried their vengeance. If any of them are caught, this could grow into a kind of vendetta. That wouldn't be likely to help anyone."

Roger's smile faded, and he made himself look severe.

"A crime has been committed, Mr Munro, and my job is to find whoever committed it. I hope you feel much better in the morning. Good night." He went out, passed the two nurses, who stared as if he was a freak, and walked along the passage to the front of the building.

He was now even more anxious to see Cartwright and the Home Office pathologist, who was probably in the middle of his job at the hospital. If the pathologist agreed with the surgeon that one of the wounds on young Grannett's head had not been caused by his fall, there was going to be a lot more to do than look for the assailants of Malcolm Munro.

He had taken to Munro, but likes and dislikes were irrelevant. What mattered was to find out how young Grannett had died, and whether there was any likelihood of murder.

It didn't surprise Roger to see a police car standing outside the office block's main entrance, with the commissionaire staring at the four tall, massive-looking men who had just got out. One was advancing, and when he saw Roger, he drew up.

"Just coming for you, Mr West. I'm Green, of the Division. I've had a word with Charley Coombs and your sergeant, so we know more or less what you want. Any special instructions?"

"We want one of the gang who attacked Munro – just one will do," Roger said mildly. "Something might have come out of the gatekeeper by now."

"Nothing doing," Green said. "These beggars climbed the fence, I doubt if anyone recognised them."

"Well, check, will you? And have the youth Woods checked, too, and all his friends, and the friends and workmates of young Grannett."

"Yes, can do." So the local man had already been well briefed.

"There's a night commissionaire on duty who might give us a lead. He slipped off just before the attack."

"I know the chap," said Green. "We'll watch him, and ask him a few questions just when he's not expecting it."

"Thanks." It was good to work with a man who didn't waste words. "Now I'm going across to my office for ten minutes, then I'm going into Elling Hospital," Roger said.

He was gone twenty minutes, and in that time managed to get a sandwich and a cup of coffee sent in from the Assembly Shop Canteen – he was famished. The last job he did was to check that the pathologist was in fact working at the hospital, with Cartwright, the local surgeon. Then he went out to his car, at a side entrance to the Assembly Shop. The quiet of the night seemed blessed after the metallic clamour inside, and Roger strolled slowly to his car, breathing in the cold night air deeply. It was not only colder but brighter; he could see most of the stars. This might mean a change in the weather, which had been poor and depressing of late. He got into the car, and drove towards the office block so as to reach the gatehouse. Malcolm Munro was coming down the steps, with Tessa Lee by his side. No one else was with them. By the foot of the steps stood a small car, the make of which Roger couldn't discern.

He heard Munro say: "If I'm not allowed to drive myself home, I'd rather be driven by you than anybody." They reached the little car. "Remind me to sell my automobile and give the proceeds to charity." He gave a little laugh, which sounded bitter. The girl didn't speak. Roger thought that in this half-light she looked even lovelier.

The commissionaire opened the door of the little car.

Roger drove ahead, was checked by two men at the gate, heard from Sheppard that so far none of the youths had been named, and then drove towards Elling. He had forgotten to ask for directions to the hospital, but that shouldn't be difficult to find. He could go back and ask the gatekeeper, or stop Munro and the girl, or inquire when he reached the main part of the suburb; the trouble was that he might have to double back on his tracks, and he didn't want to waste time.

He decided to ask the couple.

He actually slowed down, and was going to wave to them, when he realised a danger that he had completely overlooked. "Lunatic," he said to himself, quickened his speed, then took a turning to the left. The small car passed. He swung out of the turning quickly and followed it, keeping fairly close. He had no idea where Munro lived, and it was possible that they would go to the girl's home first; whether they did or not, any danger which lurked was most likely to be at Munro's home.

He should have arranged to have it watched.

He flicked on his radio, and heard a buzzing and a medley of voices, then the Information Room at the Yard.

"Chief Inspector West calling Information," he said. "Chief Inspector West calling Information."

"Information answering, Mr West. Over."

"Thank you. Request Division to have home of Mr Malcolm Munro watched immediately because of the possibility of an attack on him."

"I'll repeat that, sir ..."

When he'd heard the repeat, Roger switched off. The other car was about fifty yards ahead, and there was no other traffic on the road, but the reddish glow in the sky above Elling showed that Elling was very near, and there would be more traffic about. He drew closer, and was only twenty yards behind when the left-side indicator glowed red.

He slowed down.

They were in wide streets with large, self-contained houses on either side, obviously a residential district, as obviously one where Munro was more likely to live than the girl. Roger wondered if she had noticed that he was following, and whether she had said anything to Munro. It didn't matter. Left, right, second left; then the car slowed down again, and turned into the drive of a large house.

Roger reached the gateway a few seconds later.

The little car was pulling up outside the front door, where a bright electric light shone on the car, the pillars of the porch, the red brick. The lights glowed crimson as Tessa Lee put on the brakes: faded as she switched off the engine. Her door opened first, but before she could get round to the other side, Munro's opened.

That was when Roger saw the three men appear from some bushes behind the little car; the moment when his lapse might have been disastrous. No wonder the Yard called him lucky! He switched off his car lights, thrust the door open, slid out and left it open, so as not to slam it. As he reached the gateway, the three men were within three or four yards of the couple who were now by the side of the little car; and the men were in shadow, neither seen nor heard by Munro or the girl.

Tessa was saying: *"*No, darling, I won't come in. I couldn't face your father tonight, anyhow, and—well, it's time you had some rest, you'll be silly if you don't go to bed right away. And you shouldn't come into the office in the morning."

"Get two dozen wild horses, and see if they could keep me away," Munro said. He was standing very close to her, and Roger saw his arms go round her – and saw the nearest of the three men now almost within striking distance; he had a weapon raised, shoulder high.

"Look out!" Roger bellowed. *"Look out!"*

Munro dropped his arms almost before the first word rang out, the girl swung round, the man with the upraised weapon also spun on his toes, while the others stopped as if by clockwork, and stared over their shoulders.

"Get indoors!" Roger bellowed, and flung himself forward and grabbed at the ankles of the man nearest him. He wanted one prisoner, and it didn't matter which. He caught the ankles as the man tried to kick, and tugged hard; the man toppled down.

The others turned and ran.

Roger felt winded and bruised as he lay on the ground, but felt a kind of exultation because he had the prisoner. The man was scrabbling the gravel, but his hands and face were on the grass over which the trio had been able to approach without being heard.

Then the girl shouted: "Malcolm, don't!"

Was Munro going after the fleeing men?

Roger let his victim go, and scrambled to his feet, confident that he could stop the prisoner from getting away, prepared to be really rough if necessary. He saw Munro hurrying towards him, not towards the running men; well, that was sensible, and any help would be useful.

The man on the ground was starting to get up.

"Watch him," Roger warned, "he'll probably try to kill you if—"

He broke off.

Munro seemed to trip up, but there was little doubt that he did it purposely. He fell squarely against Roger, and his weight was enough to send Roger reeling again, off his balance at the moment of impact, Staggering, he saw the man on the ground get to his feet; before he could steady himself the man had disappeared with the others.

And Munro was saying: "I'll get him, don't worry, I'll get him!" and he turned and rushed off, as if to make it look an accident

"Malcolm!" the girl cried. "Don't go!"

Then the door opened and bright light flooded the carriage way. It shone upon Munro, who wasn't running very fast, on the girl who was half way between the car and Roger, on the gravel, the bushes, the little car itself. And it threw a shadow.

Roger didn't know for certain who it was, but felt almost sure that this was Sir Ian Munro.

Chapter Seven

Cause Of Death

Malcolm Munro did not get any farther than the gate; he stopped and swayed, as if unable to keep his balance. The girl ran towards him, passing within a foot or two of Roger and glancing at him without speaking. Roger could show his anger, but it wouldn't help. Young Munro had said that he hoped the police would not catch any of his assailants for fear of causing a vendetta, and obviously he wouldn't let much stand in the way of doing whatever he wanted.

Had he any other reason for not wanting anyone caught? Tessa Lee reached him, put her arm round his waist, and turned with him as they walked towards the door.

All this had taken only a few moments. During them, the man on the porch had stood still. Now he came stamping forward, and Roger recognised Sir Ian from a photograph. He was a head shorter than Roger, shorter still than Malcolm, but he was stocky and looked youthful; a bull of a man.

He reached Roger.

"Who are you and what are you doing here?"

"I'm Chief Inspector West, and I came to see Mr Munro got home safely," Roger said mildly.

"What's going on?" Sir Ian stared at Malcolm, who was now prominent in the porch light, saw the bandages and the scraped nose and looked astounded; so no one had told him what had happened.

"Didn't you hear me?" He gave the impression that he was trying hard not to shout. "What's going on?"

The girl said: "Sir Ian, I'm terribly sorry, but Mr Malcolm must be taken to his room. He's been hurt, and he'll collapse if we're not careful."

Sir Ian said: "So he's been hurt," and then proved to be more than a hectoring bully, for he took his son's arm, and said in a quieter voice: "Yes, I can see. Go inside, Miss Lee, and ask any servant you see to get Mr Malcolm's bed ready. Lean on me, Malcolm."

Malcolm muttered: "I'm all right."

But he wasn't; or else he was only pretending to be in a state of collapse. He didn't speak, and there seemed no doubt that he would have fallen but for his father; Roger saw that as he ran to his car, flicked on the radio, and asked the Yard to flash Division about the three assailants in this neighbourhood; it was probably too late, but he mustn't miss a chance. He hurried back, anxious to study the Chairman of Munro's, the throwback to the feudal age.

The girl had hurried ahead.

Roger reached Sir Ian in time to help the younger man up a flight of stairs which had a half-landing. The walls were painted white, and in each panel, up the staircase and in the hall, were small paintings; even the glance which Roger was able to give them told him that they were all good. He recognised a Gainsborough, thought he saw a small Rubens, was positive that a picture at the head of the staircase was by Constable. He put that out of his mind; he needed no telling that Sir Ian was a millionaire with an eye for art and a head for its values.

Then, a manservant took over.

"See that he gets to bed at once, Simm, make sure that he has everything he needs, and then come and tell me," Sir Ian said, and eyed his son as if trying to make up his mind about him. "Good night, Malcolm."

Malcolm had no colour left at all, and was breathing heavily; almost as if he had been hurt worse than anyone at the factory had suspected.

Like young Grannett?

"'Night," he said, and looked at the girl. "'Night, Tessa. Thanks."
He went with the manservant, and the girl watched every step he took, as if any pain that he felt, she felt also. Roger, deliberately silent, studied the old man's brick-red and veiny face; but had little reward. He could not read Sir Ian's expression, could not be sure what was reflected in his eyes. His voice was much quieter than it had been outside, and a little gruff.

"Come along, Miss Lee, you'll be collapsing yourself if you're not careful. Better rest before I have you sent home. Drove my son here, did you?"

She nodded.

"Come along, then." Sir Ian was brisk as he took her arm and led the way down the stairs. At the foot, he turned to look at Roger. "So you're Chief Inspector West. I hope you've already established that the death of the young man this afternoon was an accident."

"I've established that there have been two murderous attacks on your son since this afternoon," Roger said quietly, "and I want to make sure who committed them, and why."

Sir Ian stopped, stood very still, looked into Roger's eyes, kept his hold on the girl's arm, and said gratingly: "Friends of the dead youth did, of course. It is all part of the general situation, the completely unjustified revolt of employees against their employers. I want everyone involved caught and punished to the absolute extent of the law. Understand that? Everyone of them must be caught and punished."

That was followed by anticlimax, for there was a sound on the porch, as of a man hurrying. The door was now closed. The big letterbox opened, and a letter was pushed through, looking very white. The letter fell to the carpet, the letterbox clicked, the footsteps sounded again, receding.

Roger moved swiftly, reached the door and opened it, and the light fell on the face of a man who was looking over his shoulder as he hurried away.

It was Michael Grannett.

Roger said sharply: "Come here a minute!"

"Too busy," Grannett said, in a cold voice. "I've brought a note for the Chairman. I just want him to know that even though his son is a murderer, the pay claim is going to be dealt with on its merits."

Roger could have stopped him, but allowed him to hurry away; a moment after there was the sound of a motor-cycle engine, a two-stroke which seemed uneven. Roger turned back to the hall, where Sir Ian stood with the opened letter in his hand, and Tessa stood by the door looking at him almost in despair.

"May I see?" Roger asked, and took the letter when Sir Ian didn't answer. It was written in a bold hand, without flourishes, and it said simply:

> Your son may be a cold-blooded murderer, but that makes no difference to the merits of the wage claim. I hereby formally notify you that the Management's answer is expected by 5 pm on the Friday of this week, and if there is any delay the responsibility is entirely that of the Management

Roger looked up into Sir Ian's eyes; shocked yet angry eyes.

"Was that Grannett himself?"

"Yes, sir."

"I will not have that man in my factory or on my premises a moment longer than I must," Sir Ian said gratingly. "I shall dismiss him at the first opportunity, and after that he will be refused admission. If he tries to force his way in it will be trespass, and I shall charge him. I look to you to see that the law is obeyed, Mr West, and to establish *the facts*. The facts are that young Grannett's death was accidental, that he struck the first blow, and so began the fight."

There seemed hatred in the tone of his voice and in his glittering, pale-grey eyes.

Roger stayed at the house for nearly ten minutes, using every opportunity to study Sir Ian. He telephoned the Division and arranged for this house to be watched back and front, making it clear that he was preparing against the possibility of another attack on Malcolm, but Sir Ian made no comment. The Lee girl looked harassed and tired. Of one thing Roger became sure: Munro might be a throwback, might have all the qualities of an industrial dictator, but he was certainly a strong man. He had probably known exactly what he had wanted all his life, and driven ahead for it – and got it. Yet he could be gentle; he was, with Tessa Lee.

"I'm perfectly well enough to drive home myself," she said, "nothing's going to happen to me."

"I intend to make sure," Sir Ian said briefly. "I shall send—"

"Let me drive Miss Lee home," Roger offered. "You can have her car sent on later."

Sir Ian raised no objection, and Tessa's protest was perfunctory. She was anxious to leave, apparently, as if a little ill at ease in the old man's presence.

When they were outside, at Roger's car, she looked up at a lighted window, knowing that Malcolm was there.

Roger closed her door, went to the other side, and spoke to two men who got out of a police car: the Division was good and quick. There was no trace of the three assailants, he was told, before he got in beside Tessa, and said: "They'll make sure there's no more trouble, Miss Lee. Do we go anywhere near the hospital?"

"I live only five minutes' drive away from it."

"That's fine, I can call on my way back."

The girl didn't comment, and Roger waited until they reached the end of the road, and she told him which way to go. "Miss Lee," he went on very quietly, "before tonight, did you know of anyone with reason to want Mr Malcolm Munro dead?"

She seemed to be taken completely by surprise. "No, of course not."

"Do you think that these two attacks are the result of what happened this afternoon?"

"I—I'd taken it for granted that they were," she said. "Surely you don't think—" She broke off, as if struck by a new horror.

"All I can do is collect facts," Roger pointed out, quietly, "and it's a fact that I wouldn't expect two murderous attacks like this because of what happened today. A spontaneous outburst of anger, yes. One or two youngsters with a grudge, ready to throw stones and beat Mr

Munro up, yes. But there were a dozen men in the factory attack, weren't there?"

"At least."

"And three here, too. Do you know why Mr Munro deliberately helped the man I'd caught to get away?"

He sensed the way she looked at him in the darkness, caught a glimpse of the glint of her eyes as they passed a street-lamp.

"He can't have done."

She probably believed that. There was no way of being sure. She was tired and scared, and was never likely to be in a more amenable mood for being questioned. Roger had to keep reminding himself that his job was to get at the facts, to seek out criminals, to try to make sure that no more crimes were committed. He turned into the brightly lit High Street, near the Post Office where he had met Charley Coombs, and pulled up.

"I—I can get out here," Tessa said. "I'll get a bus."

"I'll drive you right home," Roger insisted, "but I may want to take you to the police station first."

"Oh, no! Surely—" she began, and broke off. She was fumbling in her bag for something. A cigarette? Roger did nothing to help her as he asked: "How long have you known Mr Malcolm Munro?"

"On—on and off for about four years."

"Socially?"

"No, hardly at all until he—he took his uncle's place, and I became his secretary. I don't think that it *matters*. I'm only his secretary."

"Listen," Roger said, and felt like a machine. "We have to have facts. His life is in danger, and it's got to be saved. He prefers to let his attackers go free, and I've got to find out why. Have I made it clear enough?—his life is in acute danger."

She said in a subdued voice: "Yes, I know."

"And you're in love with him."

"Yes." This time Roger hardly heard the word.

"So you know him well, and—"

"Not really well," she asserted. "I don't know many of his friends outside the factory. We—we aren't—"

She broke off.

She might have been going to add 'engaged' or' lovers'.

"All I want to find out is whether he has enemies, whether other attacks have been made on his life, and whether what happened this afternoon is just an excuse for these attacks, or whether they're the reason," Roger said. "Will you find out all you can, and report daily to me, until he's out of danger?"

She took the cigarette out of her case, at last, and put it to her lips. Roger lit it with his lighter, and belatedly she offered him a cigarette.

"No, thanks."

"Do you think it'll drag on and on?" she asked, almost wearily.

"The sooner I know all the facts, the sooner it will be over. Has he always had this fierce temper? "

"He's had a reputation for it."

"Has it been worse lately?"

"I don't think so."

"Has he been living under any unusual strain?"

"I wouldn't have said so."

"I want you to find out, Miss Lee," Roger said. "It might be instrumental in saving his life."

She didn't argue, but seemed to take it for granted that Roger was right. That could mean that she had reason to believe it, or that he had convinced her. But he hadn't made her talk, and hadn't eased her fears. He was quite sure she was keeping something back, as sure that it was frightening her.

She had lodgings in a big, old house, five minutes' drive from the centre of Elling. Roger saw her to the door, and as she took out her key he said abruptly: "Don't make any mistake, Miss Lee. The police want to help, and need your help to do it. What are you keeping back?"

She wasn't even surprised.

"Nothing that could make any difference," she said, and thrust open the door, on to a lighted hall, tall, dark furniture, and a tall mirror which reflected them both.

Tessa heard the door close on the Scotland Yard man, and heard him walk to his car. She stood quite still in the hall, as if physically numbed. Outside, a car door slammed and a car engine started up.

Tessa went slowly up the stairs. The landing was dark, and so was her large, high-ceilinged room. She stepped in and locked the door behind her quickly, a measure of her nervous fears. Then she saw a moving shadow, close to the wardrobe, and opened her mouth to scream; but it was the shadow of a bowl of tulips and wallflowers moved by the wind of the opening door.

On her winged dressing-table, with all the oddments of makeup and powder and creams, was a photograph of Malcolm taken only a few months ago. Across the corner it was signed: *Love, Mal*.

Love, Mal.

She wondered if he really had any idea, even now, how much she loved him. Amory had, now. Charley Coombs had, too. A lot of people would be told, but not necessarily Malcolm.

He was smiling, in that photograph.

If the brutes who had attacked him had been allowed five more minutes he might have been disfigured for life; maimed; or even dead. Yet it was the second attack which frightened her still more, with its evidence that they were likely to try and try again.

She took off her coat and hat, then put a kettle on a gas-ring. While it was coming to the boil, she slipped off her clothes, everything, and put on pyjamas and a dressing-gown. She made tea, and sat in an easy chair to drink it.

She pictured the attack in the grounds of the house again. But for the Scotland Yard detective, Malcolm would not have had a chance. Yet he had deliberately balked the detective, and let the captured assailant get away. The police would find that inexplicable, but she didn't: she believed it was because he thought he knew who was behind the attack; thought he knew who had set out to kill him.

And if he knew, she did, too.

Ought she to tell the police?

It was now nearly ten o'clock, and there was at least a chance that Roger would miss the pathologist at the hospital. That possibility made him dwell less on Tessa Lee than he had intended: he could come back to her later.

He drove fast to the hospital, parked just outside the main gates, where he could see everyone who came out, and flicked on his radio. Two cars turned into the drive of the low, flat, modern building; and another came up behind Roger. This was an ambulance. As he talked to the Yard, he saw it draw up, saw the back open, and the stretcher with a man or woman on it being lifted gently out.

He spoke to Kimbell, lately promoted to Chief Superintendent on night duty.

"Hallo, Handsome," Kimbell greeted. "I'm told your job's opening up a bit."

"I'm not sure that I like the shape or size of it," Roger said. "What I'd like is a complete dossier on Malcolm Munro and his father – in fact on all the directors of the firm, and on Colonel Harrison. The same on Michael Grannett, too – you've got him on your list, I take it."

"Yep. Both these jobs had better be handled by the morning chaps, hadn't they?"

"Get what you can for me tonight, will you?" Roger pleaded. "Especially on Malcolm Munro, and also on his secretary, plus—"

"Plus what?"

"Don't know, yet. She's Teresa Lee, Tessa for short, and lives at—" Roger gave the address rapidly, and then added: "I'd like to find something we could use to make the girl talk. I think she's scared, but she won't admit it, still less say why."

"We'll get cracking," Kimbell promised. "If she hasn't a record, the most likely bet tonight will be a newspaper or a press agency."

"I don't care where it comes from," Roger said. "I just have a feeling that there's more to this job than there seems. I'll be in about eleven." He was about to switch off when he remembered that he hadn't telephoned his own home to say he would be late. "Hey, Kimmy! Call my wife for me, will you, tell her this looks like being a midnight job."

"I'll do it right away," Kimbell promised.

"Thanks." Roger rang off, started the engine, and drove up to the front doors of the hospital. No one else had come in or out. A porter was on duty in the big hall, two others were at a reception window. He was expected, and the porter was detailed to take him to the laboratory at once.

So the pathologist and Cartwright hadn't gone.

He didn't like hospitals, but if he had to be in one, this was as good as any. Its newness was apparent, the floor was of some kind of composition which muffled sound, the doors and the elevator worked silently. A faintly astringent antiseptic smell was everywhere. He passed the door of a brightly lit room, which was swinging open, and on the door saw the word theatre. Then another door opened marked laboratory. He went in. Two white-smocked men were standing at a long, wide bench, there was all the usual paraphernalia of burettes, Bunsen burners, pipettes, test tubes, a kind of glorified school chemistry lab. Round the walls, on shelves, were specimens in glass jars; hands, fingers, toes, hearts, all kinds and sorts and sizes, all floating in spirit. He wasn't so used to this as to the general hospital atmosphere.

"Chief Inspector West, sir," announced the porter, as if he was nervous of interrupting.

The two men turned. One was Legg, perhaps the best of the younger Home Office pathologists, tall, dark-haired, with a hooked nose and the softest, gentlest pair of brown eyes in the world; a soft-voiced man, too. Next to him was a stranger, a lion of a man with a big, handsome face and a fine head of greying hair, who was stripping off rubber gloves; his hands were more the hands of a woman, the fingers long, white, beautiful.

Legg's weren't; Legg had a charwoman's hands.

"Sorry I'm late," Roger said. "This job goes deeper than it looks. Got anything for me?"

Legg said: "You don't know Mr Cartwright, do you?"

Cartwright offered his hand; not all surgeons would trouble to.

"Good evening, sir."

"So you're the great West," Cartwright said, and obviously meant the compliment; his smile was warm and friendly. "My wife tells me that some time during your investigations I've got to ask you in for a drink."

"Nice of her," Roger said. "I'd be glad to come."

"I'll keep you to that. Now—" Cartwright looked at Legg, who turned to the bench, where several photographs were lying, and where there were several tiny pieces of what looked like bloodstained bone.

"We can go back into the morgue, where we've taken him, or you can take our word and these pictures as evidence," said Legg. "There are the bruises on chin, chest, and face, commensurate with blows from a fist – very powerful blows, too, the nose is fractured." Legg was tracing marks on the photograph of young Roy Grannett, with a wholly dispassionate red forefinger. He pointed to another, of the back of the head. "Here are bruises and one slight cut, commensurate with a fall after being knocked down, and banging the head on concrete. Got that?"

"Yes." Roger was looking at a third photograph, which had been taken after the post mortem, and he hardly needed telling what was to come.

"There is a different kind of injury, caused by a single severe blow with a hammer, or some similar weapon, and it was that which caused cerebral haemorrhage, and death," said Legg. "If you follow the position of the wounds you'll see that this fatal wound was superimposed on the others. He was murdered by that blow, and it must have been delivered between the time that he was taken from the spot where they had the quarrel, and when he was collected by the ambulance and brought here."

"Positive of that," Cartwright put in.

"Quite positive."

"In other words, someone hit him after he'd been taken to the works hospital, probably hoping that it would look as if he'd died from the fall on the back of the head," Roger said almost to himself.

"That's how I add it up," Legg agreed.

It could have been done so that Malcolm Munro would be blamed for the youth's death.

Now the task was to find who had access to the factory hospital.

Chapter Eight

Hush-Hush

Roger drove through the gates at New Scotland Yard, off the Embankment, saw one constable on duty salute, and another hurry from the foot of the steps to open his door for him. He got out, and stretched; he was stiff and hungry and tired, and it was nearly half past eleven, but he couldn't go home yet.

"Better night, sir, bit cold, though."

"Could be worse," Roger said. He hurried up the steps to the main hall, and a sergeant welcomed him with a broad grin.

"Mr Kimbell in?" Roger asked.

"Haven't seen him leave, sir."

"Put me on to him," Roger said, and waited while the sergeant put a call through to the Night Superintendent. He used the time to try to get his thoughts in order, and when Kimbell spoke, said almost lightly: "Wouldn't care to have a cuppa in the canteen, would you? All I've had since midday is a couple of sandwiches."

"You go ahead, I'll join you," said Kimbell. "The steak's good tonight."

"Thanks." Roger rang off and went to the canteen. It was nearly empty; the main mealtime for the night staff was between twelve and one o'clock. He ordered a steak, knowing that it would be cooked exactly as he liked it, and resisted the temptation to nibble at some bread. He was still waiting when Kimbell came in, a tall, nearly whitehaired man, whose face belied the hair; he looked no more than forty-five. He was thin and rather angular, and his grin was friendly to all and sundry.

He came and sat down opposite Roger.

"What are you going to have?" Roger asked.

"Coffee, but I'll wait," said Kimbell. "What's all this about murder?"

Roger explained ...

"Couldn't have it more positive than that," said Kimbell. "What do you make of it?" He had a genius for getting other people to talk, and also for picking out the salient points of a story.

"I may be wrong, but I think the way these two attacks were made on young Munro suggests something deeper than vengeance consequent upon today's shindy," Roger said. "As if the assailants had been put up to it. But I could be fooling myself." He sat back as his steak arrived, sizzling, a heap of chipped golden brown potatoes with it. "Looks fine, Ted, thanks," he said to the man who brought it. "Two coffees now, please." He waited for Ted to go, and then added: "I think someone hates Malcolm Munro's guts, and saw a golden chance to get him charged with manslaughter, and perhaps wreck his whole future at Munro's. But it could go deeper still. It could be that someone is out to wreck Munro's, at least to the length of stopping them from getting their Mark 9 on to the export market."

"Hmm."

"Don't you agree?"

"Haven't enough evidence to agree or disagree," said Kimbell, "but if I were laying money, it would be on you. You want: *(a)* someone who hates Malcolm Munro, and *(6)* someone who hates the whole set-up there."

Roger cut into the steak, and it could not have been more tender.

"With especial attention to Michael Grannett, and an eye on the Lee girl, who might know the very thing we need."

"Grannett's the strong candidate for hater-in-chief and troublemaker *in excelsis,"* Kimbell observed, and so proved how thoroughly he had studied the reports which had been sent through only an hour or so ago. "Haven't got anything on him yet, except that he's worked at Munro's for twelve years and been a thorn in the flesh all the time. But I've got something for you on the other one, part (a) as it were."

Roger stopped eating.

"Enemy of Malcolm Munro?"

"Yep."

"Don't hold out on me."

"Fellow by the name of Hugh Torrance," Kimbell said, and did not even show how much he relished the revelation. "You've heard of him. Chief test driver of Munro's for the past ten years or so, probably one of the finest drivers in the country. Remember?"

"Of course I know of Torrance. What makes him Munro's enemy?"

"Two things. First, Torrance was almost set for a seat on the Board, until Munro decided to go on. There's a story that now that Munro's on, Torrance never will be, because of his antipathy. Second, a girl named Teresa Lee. The trouble with you is second sight."

Roger, who had started to eat again, put his knife and fork down, and said: "That's right, spoil my steak. Give."

"Same source of information is a motoring correspondent of the *Globe*," Kimbell told him. "It seems that Torrance and Tessa Lee were very good friends at one time; in fact, engaged. That lasted until about three weeks after Munro became a director. Then she broke off the engagement. The following night, Torrance picked a quarrel with Munro at a small drinking club, exclusive to the motoring set. Dozens of witnesses. Munro tried to stop it from developing into a brawl, but finally there was one."

"Who won?"

"Munro cut Torrance into little pieces. Munro is just about the best heavyweight to come out of Oxford in the past fifty years, it seems. How does it sound?" Kimbell was smug.

"It sounds as if you've got someone looking for Torrance and checking into his recent activities," said Roger, and started on his steak again.

"I've two men doing it, but like the other things, it'll probably have to wait till morning," Kimbell said. "Never know what turns up if you dig a little hole in dirt, do you?"

"Think Tessa Lee knows about this?" Roger asked.

"She was present when the fight took place. Torrance was drunk. He's not much of a drinker, can't hold his liquor."

"Well, well," said Roger. "I had a feeling she was holding something back tonight. Do you happen to know if Torrance was on duty at the factory this afternoon?"

"Yes, he was getting a Mark 9 ready for a test run tomorrow, when there's a party of big export buyers due to see a demonstration."

Roger finished a mouthful of steak, and then deliberately cut another piece off without looking at the Night Superintendent, but he said: "You are about to explode a bombshell. What?"

"Torrance had a slight spill on the trial track this afternoon. About two fifteen. He went to the works hospital for attention. In his overalls. Carrying his tools. Including a spanner. Like me to bring him in for you?"

"No," said Roger very softly, "not yet. It's almost too perfect. Right man, right place, right weapon – too much for coincidence. Kimmy, do you know what I'd do if I were the boss around here?"

"Yes," said Kimbell, promptly. "You would treat the news of the murderous blow on Grannett's head as hush-hush until we've had time to look round a bit more, and get some more facts assembled. If the killer thinks we've been fooled, he'll feel so good that he might get a little careless."

"Thanks," said Roger warmly. "Recommend it in your chit to Knightley in the morning, will you?"

"Yes. My Gawd," exclaimed Kimbell, noticing Roger's plate, "if I put away a meal as fast as that I'd have indigestion for a week." He took a cup of coffee from Ted, and went on: "Why don't you have baked jam roll or plum duff or something equally light for sweet?"

"What have you got, Ted?" Roger asked.

"As a matter of fact, sir, the baked jam roll's still on."

"Fine."

"Double portion, as usual?"

"Please, and don't forget the extra jam."

"I give in," Kimbell marvelled, "I give in. This must be where you get your reserves of strength from, Handsome. Anything else you want?"

"Yes, please, sir," said Roger humbly. "A couple of men out at the factory tonight, to work there – here's the key to the office they've put at our disposal. And a recommendation for a clerk – one of the older men will do – and a couple of good detective officers at the factory by eight o'clock in the morning."

"Going to make that your HQ?" Kimbell mused. "Probably a good idea. OK. Well, I've got to go up to the office, you may not believe it, but there are other bad men about tonight. The worst job we've had is an old chap nearly battered to death at Highgate. I'm expecting the swine who did it in any minute. Here's a note of what we've done for you, you can put it under your pillow, and if you have a nightmare, don't blame anything but your greed."

Roger took a slip of paper.

"Kimmy," he said, "there ought to be more like you. Thanks."

"Think nothing of it," Kimbell said, and went off. Roger studied the list, and began to smile. It was a summary of everything which he had recommended from the time he had reached Munro's factory, and it included reports from the Division. Sir Ian's house was being watched, back and front, three youths suspected of taking part in the first attack on Munro had been questioned and released because there was no proof, oddments of clues had been found at the scene of the attack, but nothing really helpful had yet come from them. There were notes on a report from Coombs, two on reports from Sheppard, and a note that Kimbell had told Sheppard to go off duty at ten-forty. In brackets were the words: *He wanted to wait for you, Handsome. Wouldn't let him.* There were details about Torrance, too. If Tessa Lee believed that Torrance had become so deadly an enemy, it would explain why she had pretended to know nothing.

If Malcolm Munro, undoubtedly capable of a kind of twisted quixotism, believed the attacks had been inspired by Torrance, but didn't want it proved, it was easy to understand why he had let that man escape.

There were many undercurrents, too, among them the tension between Mike Grannett and the management, which had lasted for at least twelve years.

Roger went up to his office, and spent three-quarters of an hour writing out a report for Knightley and the Assistant Commissioner, and making a list of the inquiries he wanted started first thing in the morning. Time would be invaluable.

Then he went to his home in Bell Street, Chelsea; a small, detached, inner suburban house in a quiet street, where only the lamps were alight, and all the houses were in darkness. He drove the car into the garage, the doors of which had been left open for him; Scoopy and Richard, his two children, would have seen to that. He closed the garage doors softly, and opened the front door of the house, listened for the slightest sound, and heard none. He yawned, relaxed and tired now that the tensions of the day were past, and didn't even go into the kitchen. His wife had probably left some sandwiches out, but it was a household rule that if he didn't eat them, one of the boys would take them for lunch next day.

He went upstairs, the only light coming from a street-lamp shining through the landing window. He opened the boys' door, heard their soft breathing and could just make out their heads against the pillow. Peace at thirteen and fourteen. He could see that Scoopy's big body was askew, and Richard nearly hidden under the bedclothes. He closed the door quietly, went into his own bedroom, and undressed by the light of that friendly street-lamp. Janet didn't stir until he got into bed. She was very warm. He pushed the eiderdown back, and she moved and grunted a little, and then quite suddenly asked in a clear voice:

"Are you in bed?"

"Yes, sweet."

"Good night"

"Good night." Roger felt sure that she was asleep almost before the response was out.

He lay on his back for a while, letting thoughts of what had happened trickle through his mind, still working on the problem, still wondering how deep it would go. There were cases which were easy from the start, and there were others which promised, even in the first hour or two, to be as stubborn as any could be. The truth about the Munro job was that he did not yet understand the tensions and emotions under the surface. He doubted whether anyone was telling the whole truth.

He went to sleep.

He woke a little after eight Janet was downstairs, and he could hear the boys in the garden; every now and again there was the sneezing sound of Martin-called-Scoopy's airgun, and the clatter of a tin-can whenever a slug caught it. Roger wondered if a similar noise had woken him, smiled lazily, yawned and stretched, and then heard Janet walking to the foot of the stairs. She called in a voice pitched low enough not to wake him.

"Want a cup of tea yet, Roger?"

"Sounds wonderful!"

In a moment she came hurrying up, and he knew that she was as eager to see him as she had been sixteen years ago, when they had been newlyweds; and he was as glad to see her. At forty, her dark hair was marked with only a little grey, her eyes and mouth showed hardly a wrinkle, her complexion was as fresh as a girl's. She was wearing a transparent plastic apron over a white blouse and dark-green skirt, and carrying a big cup of tea and the newspapers. She put these down and sat on the edge of the bed; it was good to kiss her.

"Did you get my message?"

"Yes, when I'd given up hope!"

"How're the boys?"

"They want to get off early, there's some kind of racing practice before school, so they're going to have breakfast while you're shaving." That was good, for it gave him and Janet twenty minutes on their own. "I'll send them up to say goodbye," Janet went on, and got up with obvious reluctance. "If I don't go, they'll be late. Are you in a hurry this morning?"

"Ought to leave before nine," Roger said ruefully.

"And not home until two, I bet!" But she was not vexed, not even disappointed, so she had expected it

Roger sipped the tea and opened the newspapers, including the *Globe* and the *Wire*. It didn't surprise him to see his own and Malcolm Munro's face staring up at him, Munro's an excellent studio portrait taken quite recently. There was a smaller picture of Roy Grannett, too, looking very young.

When he had lain unconscious or dozing on a bed of sanctuary, someone had crept in and smashed a murder weapon down on his skull.

The story, though not yet one of murder, had been given big treatment. There was a sketch of the Mark 9, and a brief story of its sweeping successes on the export market, but the main story was of the wage-demand meeting, the fight, and the death of the youth. Nothing hinted that there had been any other cause of death. The *Wire* discussed objectively whether this would be a charge of manslaughter, and mentioned almost in passing that murder was ruled out.

On the whole, the newspapers were neutral.

The boys came hurrying upstairs, Martin nearly five feet ten tall, with a broad, smiling face and eager eyes; Richard a head shorter at the age of thirteen, slighter, with ears which stuck out rather, but gave his equally eager face a kind of piquancy. They were excited about the strike news and the case Roger was on, especially details of the cars. Had he seen them being made? Had he seen any of the new Mark 9s? Had he seen the *marvellous* test driver, Torrance? Then Janet called them from downstairs, and reluctantly they left.

The house seemed very quiet when they had gone.

Did the Grannett household feel the same kind of quiet? Or was there real grief in that ordinary little home?

Roger reached the Yard at a quarter past nine, threw 'good mornings' right and left, and bustled along to his own office, anxious to find out which of his recommendations had been acted upon, and which had been referred back for discussion. It was too early to expect many fresh reports in yet, but he was always hopeful for miracles.

A glance at the notes on his desk showed that Knightley had agreed with all of his main recommendations. Three extra men were already at the factory, and Sheppard had gone there to brief them. No Superintendent could have been better served. The Yard was digging deep into the pasts of young Munro, the girl, Torrance, and Grannett. Nothing had come in about any of Munro's assailants; it was quite possible that they would draw a blank.

But there was a report, telephoned from the factory by Charley Coombs, giving the names of the people known to have been in the hospital and having access to the room where the boy had lain, at the time that he had been there. Roger studied the list.

Torrance he knew about; he had been there for twenty minutes. Amory didn't surprise him. Colonel Harrison did. Michael Grannett had been to see his brother; in fact had been at the hospital all the time, but out of the room for ten minutes or more. Those ten minutes might prove to be the vital time factor.

Who else?

Malcolm Munro had been there, too. There was one note which Roger read twice.

Malcolm M. did not report to the Day Sister, but was seen to enter the hospital and the room where the injured man lay. He was seen to leave five minutes afterwards. He did not report to the receptionist, and entered and left by a side door.

Chapter Nine

The Test Driver

Roger called at the Divisional Headquarters on his way to the factory, but there was no further news. The Detective Inspector, Green, was on duty, and said that he would be at the factory within an hour. He was curious about the reason for extra Yard men being sent, but Roger didn't tell him about the pathologist's report, not wanting too many to know about it for the time being. Torrance was due to make a test run at ten-fifteen, and Roger was anxious to be there, to judge the man's equality before questioning him.

Roger was admitted by the gatekeeper, and given a brisk good morning. The place, which had seemed so strange the previous day, now had a familiar look, and was much brighter because the sun was out. The massed cars no longer seemed derelict, but to be standing ready for cellulosing; as they were. There was a briskness about the way people moved. The boxes cordoning off the spot where young Grannett had lain had been removed; but there was a biggish patch cordoned off with stakes and ropes outside the office building. Malcolm Munro's maroon-and-grey Rolls-Bentley was outside, so were several other expensive cars. Just inside the gates were hundreds of old battered cars, some new, tiny and shiny, hundreds of motor-cycles and motor-scooters, thousands of bicycles.

A little group of men, obviously executives, were moving from a corner of the white office block; they disappeared. Roger drove to the corner and saw them going through a gate in a high fence; there he heard the roar of an engine, so loud that it might have been that of an aircraft, not a motor car. A big sign on the fence read:

> testing ground
> keep out

Would Torrance be driving yet?

Roger waited until the group had gone through the gateway, recognising Amory, Harrison, and Malcolm Munro among them, and got out of the car. He wasn't surprised to see Charley Coombs waving to him from a spot half way across the yard to the Assembly Shop, and he waited, lighting a cigarette and enjoying the sunshine; it was ten degrees warmer this morning than it had been yesterday.

Coombs looked very bright and clear-eyed, and more youthful looking than many men still at the Yard; a grey-haired cherub.

"'Morning, Handsome, want to go and see the fun?"

"Try-out on, yet?"

"Torrance is going to give one of his demonstrations, and there are two Americans and a Swede among the prospective customers touring the factory today, so it'll be good."

"Anything need doing in my office?" Roger asked.

"No. Your army's there, Sheppard's out and about, trying to get a line on young Munro's attackers. He's going round the factory with three or four Divisional chaps."

"All right, we'll see what happens after Torrance tries to break his neck," Roger said, and they fell into step and went towards the testing-ground gate. "Thanks for your reports, Charley, they're worth a small fortune."

"Want to know something?" Coombs was looking straight ahead.

"Always willing to learn."

"Torrance is drunk," Coombs said.

Roger saw the test driver standing in front of a standard Mark 9, a sleek, slim-looking semi-sports car, very low on the ground. The group of men were approaching him, tall, well-dressed, with Malcolm Munro talking to one of the Americans, whose voice floated back in a pleasing southern drawl. There were two repair pits on this large private track, and some low buildings, a petrol tender, and a single petrol pump. Two or three mechanics stood about. Only the one car was in sight. Torrance was getting into this. At a distance, he seemed little more than a boy; in fact, he was in the middle thirties, slim, with dark curly hair, looking more like a southern European than an Englishman. He waved as he dropped into his seat,

Roger said: "You sure he's drunk?"

"As near as I can be."

"Does Munro know it?"

"I don't talk to the Munros of this world unless they talk to me."

"If Torrance is drunk he mustn't drive," Roger said. "Tell Munro that I want a word with him urgently, will you?" He left Coombs, and hurried towards the track; only a concrete ridge separated it from the uneven grassland of the enclosure. He ignored a shout from a mechanic and a wave from Torrance. The engine was roaring again, and as the man opened the throttle, the air seemed to quiver. A mechanic came running, waving a flag at him, to get off the track. He ignored the man, and ran straight towards the waiting car. By that time, Coombs had reached Munro. All of the party was standing still and staring towards Roger, doubtless thinking him mad. Then, Torrance started the car.

He was fifty yards away, and Coombs said that he was drunk. He was alone in that car, which could travel at a hundred and thirty miles an hour. The bright sunlight shone on it, making it look as if it were painted in blood. The engine roared and then settled down to a steadier note. The wheels began to turn, and the car headed straight for Roger. The mechanic stood only ten yards away, off the actual track, and now his words could be heard: he was almost shrieking: "Get to hell out of here! Get off the track!"

Roger slowed down to a brisk walk. The car was less than thirty yards away now, and still moving slowly, but it had tremendous acceleration, and Torrance was magnificent at the wheel. Now, Munro was also waving and shouting something, but he was farther away.

Roger semaphored with his arms, for Torrance to stop. There was still good time, but it didn't look as if the man meant to obey. He was a daredevil at the best of times, and if he was really drunk, would probably accept this challenge and rely on the car and the roaring engine to make Roger give way. Roger didn't slacken his pace any more. He reckoned the chances of making a leap to the right or left; if he had to jump for it, he would go to the left, where the grass verge was nearer. His heart was thumping; he wasn't enjoying this, but if he gave way now his stock at the factory would drop to zero; a dozen men were watching, and the story would spread like wildfire.

Ten yards.

The engine roared deafeningly; frighteningly. Roger missed a step. He could see Torrance's screwed-up face, could see the glittering bright blue eyes behind the curved windscreen. If he did come on faster—

The car stopped.

Roger put a hand to his forehead, felt the sweat, but didn't wipe it off. He was only five yards away from the red beauty, meeting Torrance's angry glare. Men came running towards him, and he believed that one of them was Malcolm, although he couldn't be sure. Mechanics were coming from the pits, too, but it was the test driver who jumped out of the car in a single, sweeping movement, slammed the door and reached him first.

"What the hell do you think you're doing? Who the devil do you think you are?"

Drunk?

Undoubtedly whisky was strong on his breath, and it wasn't yet half past ten. His speech was a little slurred, if hardly that of a drunk man; but a drunk could sober up very quickly.

Now Malcolm arrived, walking the last few yards, breathing a little heavily. His lip was still swollen and his right hand was bandaged.

"Take it easy, Hugh," he said, and might have been talking to his best friend. The calmness of his voice proved that he had his temper under rigid control. "This is Chief Inspector West of Scotland Yard."

"I don't care a damn whether he's the Commissioner at the Yard and Mr Home Pomposity rolled into one, if he gets in my way again when I'm on the track I'll run him down first and see who he is afterwards." Torrance was very pale, and his eyes still glittered; there was no friendliness in his voice or manner when he glanced at Munro. "Get him off the track. I'm supposed to be showing the foreign gentlemen what the car can do."

"Before you drive round, Mr Torrance, I'd like a word with you," Roger said, and glanced at Munro. "In private, if that's all right with you."

Munro didn't speak, but looked at Torrance almost as if with appeal. Three mechanics were out of earshot, waiting for instructions and surprised that they hadn't yet been given. The group of buyers stood a little way off, watching silently. Coombs was near them.

"Well, it isn't all right with me," Torrance growled. "Get off the track, copper."

"Hugh, Mr West is in charge of investigations into Roy Grannett's death."

Torrance flashed round at him.

"He's in charge of finding out what started the fight in which you killed young Grannett, and if he's any questions to ask, why doesn't he ask you? I wasn't present. If I had been, I would probably have broken your neck." Torrance glowered at Roger. "You going to get out of my way or not?"

"Mr Torrance," Roger asked, without raising his voice, "how long were you with Grannett in the hospital yesterday afternoon?"

Torrance seemed to shake, as under an impact.

It was impossible to judge Munro's reaction, but Roger had an impression that he was surprised. There were several seconds of silence, during which Torrance seemed to be fighting for self-control. He was handsome in his dark, Sicilian way, and his manner suggested that he also had trouble with his temper.

Tessa Lee seemed to attract men like that.

"Well?" Roger asked. "How long, Mr Torrance?"

An answer came angrily.

"Two or three minutes, that's all, but what the hell difference does that make?"

"Was he conscious?"

"He looked in a damned bad way to me."

"Was he conscious?"

"He didn't speak to me, if that's what you mean. What are you driving at?"

"There might be reason to believe that Grannett was encouraged to pick a quarrel with Mr Munro, and if he was, I want to know who encouraged him. Did he talk to you, Mr Torrance?"

"No."

"Did you know him?"

Torrance didn't answer.

"He wouldn't be likely to know one of the Assembly Shop apprentices," Munro put in.

He did everything he could to ease the situation for Torrance, but every time he spoke, Torrance seemed to spark. Now, he glared at Munro and said roughly: "That shows how much you know about what goes on in your own factory. Young Roy was a damned good mechanic, and he wanted to come into the pits and work for me. I saw a lot of him. Tried him out, too. In a few months' time he would have been one of my crew."

"So you knew him well?" Roger said.

"Well enough to wish the man who killed him to hell!"

Munro didn't speak.

"Did he tell you that someone had persuaded him to pick a quarrel with Mr Munro?" Roger insisted.

"No, he didn't. And I don't believe he would pick a quarrel with anyone unless there was a good reason for it. They don't come any better than young Roy. If someone's sold you the idea that he was paid to pick a quarrel, forget it I thought you were a good detective," he added with a sneer. "That's the kind of story you'd expect to hear about him now – it's the only way that Munro could establish the so-called fact that Roy started the fight, and the only way he can creep out of a manslaughter charge. Wouldn't you spread that canard if you were in danger of being sent to gaol for a couple of years?"

"Was anyone else with you when you saw Grannett at the hospital yesterday afternoon?"

"No."

"Did you see anyone else go into him, after you'd left?"

"Yes, I saw *him*." Torrance poked a thumb towards Munro. "And I met Roy's brother outside, he said that he was going to see him, too. And that's the last word I'm going to say to you today, copper. I'm going to drive that car or else I'm going to throw my hand in."

Munro said: "Is there any objection to Mr Torrance driving now?"

"No," said Roger coldly. "Provided he's sober enough."

Torrance swung round and went back to the car, waving the mechanics away. Roger turned with Munro towards the grass at the side of the track, and as he went, he asked very quietly, making sure that his words didn't carry: "Does Torrance always drink before driving?"

Munro missed a step. "Of course he doesn't."

"He'd soaked up plenty this morning," Roger pointed out. They stepped on to the grass, and the engine started up again, roaring. "Did you know that someone had put Roy Grannett up to picking a quarrel, Mr Munro?"

"It hadn't occurred to me."

"If it's true, do you know who might have fixed it?"

"I can't even believe it's true."

"Mr Munro," Roger said, clearly enough for Munro to hear every word, "last night you helped one of your assailants to escape. This morning, you've done all you can to protect Torrance, who is known to be ill-disposed towards you. Your life is obviously in danger. What makes you behave so handsomely towards your enemies?"

Munro didn't answer.

They stood with their backs to the small group, and watched the car as it roared past; its engine gradually quietened, and it was easier to hear themselves speak while watching the scarlet streak at one of the steeply banked corners of the track.

Then Munro said: "Hugh Torrance isn't an enemy of mine, Mr West. He is my closest friend. He's had a difficult time emotionally, and gets easily upset. You annoyed him. As for anyone picking a quarrel with me – no, I can't see why they should. I don't believe anyone did. Now if you'll forgive me I ought to get back to the others, they are overseas buyers likely to place large orders for the Mark 9."

"What will happen if there's a strike?" Roger demanded abruptly.

"I don't think there is going to be any strike," Munro responded. "There won't be if I can stop it." He gave a quick, unamused smile, and added: "You will excuse me, won't you?" and went striding off to join the two Americans, Harrison and the Swede. Coombs still stood by. The car had completed one circuit, and the noise was deafening again as it hurtled past. At the nearest corner it looked as if it would be bound to go over the top. Instead, it roared down into the straight again. Then Torrance began to stunt, sending the car at a hundred and twenty miles an hour, swerving and swinging about, as if intent on causing a spill. Roger was nearer the group now, and heard the Swede say in excellent English: "Well, it has quite remarkable road-holding qualities, that I must agree."

"It's almost impossible to turn it over," Munro said, "and it's as safe at corners as anything on four wheels."

Torrance had settled down again. For a moment, on a corner, it looked as if the car was heading straight for them, but it changed direction swiftly and hurtled along the straight. The engine roar was harsh with menace. It made another complete circuit, and that was when Roger noticed a change in Munro's manner, saw him looking at the scarlet streak as if anxiously. The mechanics were standing more tensely, too. There had been no change in the roar of the engine, no indication of trouble that Roger could see, but these experts suddenly felt anxious. Harrison's colourless face betrayed the same anxiety.

The Colonel held a stop-watch.

He glanced at it.

"He's going too fast," he said, as if to himself. "A hundred and thirty-five is asking for trouble. Asking for trouble."

So that was it. Torrance was in sole control and was driving the car faster than it had ever been driven before. The Munro men had expected him to slow down, but he showed no signs of doing so. He rose up a banked corner so fast that it seemed impossible for him to keep on the road. Munro and Harrison held their breath, one of the Americans shut his eyes, the Swede seemed to be muttering under his breath. But the car flew along the upper edge of the track, and then swept down again.

Roger felt sweat breaking out over his forehead, and had no doubt that the others felt the same.

Surely Torrance would slow down now.

He did not,

"For God's sake, Hugh!" Munro gasped, as if the driver could hear.

Then Harrison said: "Get away from here. This way, all of you, hurry," He pushed the Swede and an American towards the pits, the other American and Roger followed, but Malcolm Munro stood where he was.

"Malcolm, come on!" Harrison shouted.

The roar of the engine drowned the words so far as Roger was concerned. Munro held his ground. Harrison still hustled the others off. Roger saw that the Mark 9 was on the banked corner closest to them again, and this was the spot where, on the last circuit, it had looked as if the car was coming off the track towards them, but where it had straightened up.

Would it this time?

It hustled down the slope, and was heading straight for Malcolm Munro. Roger was twenty yards away from him, the others twenty yards farther away. Harrison was shouting something, but the only sound was that of the roaring engine, screaming as if it were a dive bomber.

Then the car left the track.

Chapter Ten

Crash

There was danger for them all. If the car overturned there was no telling where it might fling itself, no telling where wreckage might fly. Now it was just a scarlet blur, not far from Roger. He saw a dozen things at the same time. The face of the driver, twisted either in fear or in fury, hands tight on the wheel. Munro leaping away from the oncoming terror, trying to save himself. Harrison and the watching party, eyes rounded and mouth agape. The mechanics, two of them running, two others, whom he hadn't seen before, climbing into a little fire-fighting jeep which had been standing by. Of all these things, the most vivid was the red streak. This was now so blurred that Roger could no longer see the face of the driver, could only just make out the shape of his head.

As the car passed Munro it struck a hole in the ground, lurched, seemed to be flopping over on one side, then suddenly turned almost a complete circle, and headed back towards the track. Could Torrance hold it? Had he done this deliberately, to frighten rather than to kill?

The car gave a sickening lurch and turned a complete somersault; once, twice, thrice.

Then it seemed to fall apart.

Roger thought: 'He can't live through it, he's killed himself,' and stood oblivious of danger as the fragments flew off the car; wheels, pieces of metal and glass, smaller oddments all crashed about him, but none touched him. He expected the car to burst into flames, but it didn't. He was nearest; and the jeep was rapidly catching him. Then he saw that Torrance was half out of the driving-seat, that a door was open but jammed against the ground so that there was no room for Torrance to get out even if he had the strength. The driver's eyes were open, his face was that of a man in agony.

Roger had a split second to decide whether to defy the risk of an explosion.

He saw the jeep jolting to a standstill as he sprang forward, reaching Torrance and the car before anyone else. If he could ease it up a little, Torrance might be able to crawl out; it was useless pulling at the man. He saw the bright blood on Torrance's forehead and chin, and the desperate appeal in the blue eyes. He reached the car, breathed in the reek of petrol, felt roasted by the heat which seemed to promise a sudden explosion. The car was a lightweight; he simply got his shoulder beneath the body close to the partly open door, and heaved. Lightweight? He felt as if there were tons of metal on top of him, and the smell of petrol was much stronger; choking. He heard a crackling sound, too, and the noise of Torrance breathing. Then a man appeared by his side, saying: "Hold the strain a minute." This was a mechanic, who was on one knee, trying to pull Torrance out. There followed a hissing sound; another mechanic was playing a fire extinguisher over the car. Roger gritted his teeth and heaved, and the car went back an inch or two. The wheels were off and the broken hubs were deep in the ground, that was why he had such difficulty in getting it up. Another man appeared by his side, facing him, bent down and did exactly the same thing as he.

Munro.

"Both together," Munro said clearly. "I'll call three. One—two—*three.*"

They heaved. The car lifted. The mechanic dragged Torrance free and then to a safe distance. One of the Americans arrived and took some of the strain while Roger and Munro got clear. The car thumped and rattled back on its side. The extinguisher was still hissing. Another car engine sounded, and when Roger glanced towards the gate he saw that it was a white ambulance, with

Coombs clinging to a door. Dozens of people were streaming through the gateway, there was to be another major sensation. He muttered: "How is he?"

"Looks as if his legs got it," Munro said. "I—" He broke off, hesitated, and then said: "If he lives, he'll have to thank *you*."

Roger managed a grin.

"Pleasure," he said. "Thank God the thing didn't blow up." Then he asked, while everything was still sharp and raw in Munro's mind, "Do you think he did it deliberately? Did he mean to kill himself and take you with him?"

"It was an accident," Munro said, but he looked shaken and ill. "It must have been an accident; it must have been."

An hour later, Roger walked through the Assembly Shop, and this time practically every worker at the conveyors stopped to look round at him. It coincided with a morning break, and a little group of people, mostly youngsters and girls, were gathered round a tea trolley. One of them called out: "Good show, Inspector!" and there was a spontaneous outburst of applause. That was pleasant. In some ways, the past hour had been, too: an hour when Roger had been able to bask in a kind of glory. In it, he might easily have forgotten that he was here to find a murderer. Worse, he had warmed to the management because of their obvious gratitude, and the way in which he had been accepted. Not patronised, accepted. He had been in the directors' room at the main office building, with Sir Ian, Robert Amory, Harrison, A. C. Cobb, and several others, all falling over themselves to express their gratitude, to assure him that there was nothing they wouldn't do to help, and had left just before the first of the newspapermen had arrived. Soon there would be swarms.

He must be very careful indeed on this tight-rope. If the workers once thought he was pro-management he could do a great deal of harm, and his present popularity made the potential harm greater.

It would not take much to make a strike inevitable, and he knew that if it came, it would be long and bitter. If he kept his head and an even balance he might be able to help prevent the stoppage; so there were two sides to the job.

Sheppard was coming towards him.

"Thanks," Roger called to the little group, and waited until Sheppard drew up. "Lucky thing young Munro had the guts to weigh in," he said to the sergeant, "I'd be a goner if he hadn't." He appeared to be addressing Sheppard, but everyone nearby heard, although no one commented; the words would sink in, getting thoughts under firmer control.

"How's Torrance?" Sheppard asked, smoothing his bald head, a mannerism which betrayed excitement of some kind. They were nearing the office.

"The factory doctor thinks it's a matter of broken legs and a few cuts and bruises, but he's not sure yet," Roger said. "He should come through."

"Think he did try to kill Munro?"

"Who suggested that?" Roger was sharp.

"It's all over the place," Sheppard said, and grinned a little too broadly, no doubt uneasily, as if he feared that Roger really disapproved. "It's known that Torrance and Munro haven't exactly been bosom friends recently. Started with the Lee girl breaking off her engagement to Torrance."

Roger said with a resigned grimace: "This place is like a village."

"Oh, well, that's nice and neighbourly. Had any reward for your labours?"

Sheppard asked that as he opened the office door. An elderly man with surprisingly dark hair got up from a desk which had been brought in since last night. He was a heavy, rather ponderous-looking individual, with tired grey eyes.

"Hallo, Pop." Roger nodded to him. "Sit down, and keep at it."

'Pop' obeyed. His nickname did not imply age, but was a shortened form of the surname: Popham. Roger had known him for years as a painstaking keeper of records with a sound memory: exactly the right man to take notes and telephone messages, and to study and correlate them. He seldom had much to say for himself.

"You had any luck?" Roger asked Sheppard.

"I think I could name two of the men who attacked Munro here last night, an Arthur Winn and a Robert Pegnall," Sheppard said. "They were seen climbing the fence not far from the gatehouse by a night-watchman. But I can't prove it, and there's nothing we could use for a charge. I've sent Tilbury and Marino, the DOs from the Yard—good pair, sir, the Yard's looking after us!—to pick up more information if they can. They're out in the shops, trying to get the oddments found last night identified."

"Such as?"

"A penknife, a ballpoint pen, a handkerchief, and a comb." Sheppard was briskly factual. "Our chaps are especially after the two main suspects, Winn and Pegnall. If we can prove their ownership of any of the exhibits, they'd pay for questioning again."

"Do they work here?"

"Yes – both night-shift labourers." Sheppard pointed to a note on the desk. "There are the addresses."

"Right," said Roger. "Have 'em picked up, but don't do it anywhere near the factory. You'd better take 'em to the Yard for questioning, that might put the wind up them more than if you talk to them here or at the Division. I'll talk to them myself, if they don't make a confession! All we want is to know who put them up to the attack on Munro, and whether they know anything about the second attack – and can they name any one of the three who made it? Got all that?"

"Yes, sir."

"We can keep the 'sir' until someone else is in earshot. Anything special in about Michael Grannett?"

"There's a kind of case history here," Sheppard said, "and Mr Knightley rang up to say he's sending over a dossier on everyone concerned."

"Fine. What's the mood of the workers this morning?"

"I'd say it's mixed," answered Sheppard reflectively. "Old Charley Coombs has been listening wherever he could, and has several factory policemen under him, who mix with the men. On the whole, I'd say it was fifty-fifty – half saying that Munro killed young Grannett and ought to be sent to gaol, the other half saying that

Grannett started it, it was just an accident. There's only one thing that's really general."

"What's that?"

"Woods, the orange-thrower, has been reinstated, and everyone sees that as a defeat for the management. Funny thing, but young Munro made more enemies because he made Woods collect his cards than he did because Roy Grannett died."

"Anything new on the Grannett family?"

"Michael is married, two children, pretty wife, house divided into two flats, the mother and young boy lived at the top. The mother's pretty cut up, I'm told."

"I can believe it," Roger said. "Have you seen Michael Grannett this morning?"

"Yes, in the Paint Shop, where he's foreman."

"I think I'll go and see him," Roger said. "You go and work with Tilbury and Marino, get after those two night-shift labourers, and go and see young Woods, too. If Roy Grannett stood up for him so quickly, they may have been good friends. Tell me what you make of him, before I see him myself."

"Right," said Sheppard.

An hour before Roger had given those instructions young Woods left his mother's little house in the poorer part of Elling, and, edgy and nervous, went to a café where he often met Roy and his other friends. He had a sick kind of feeling whenever he thought of Roy being dead.

Woods had not much of a mind, and his thoughts were mostly sensuous or emotional. Now he was scared, because he believed that Roy's death had been murder. He even knew what weapon had been used, and felt sure he knew who had used it.

As he drew near the cafe he saw two men loitering outside: two night-shift labourers at the plant. They were looking at him in an odd way, and that made his mood of nervous tension even worse.

They barred his way into the café.

"Going somewhere, Woody?" That was a man named Winn.

"I—I'm just going to get a cuppa, that's all, no harm in that, is there?"

Winn took his arm tightly.

"Thought you preferred oranges, Woody!" He was a big, tough-looking, brutish man, with a powerful grip. "How about coming and having a slap-up vegetarian's dinner with us, eh? It'll be our treat."

"No! My ma expects me back soon, I mustn't." There was no outward reason for it, but Woods felt the hold of terror upon him. "Let me go."

"Aw, come on," Winn said, and twisted Woods' wrist enough to make him wince. "That hurt? You won't get hurt if you do what we tell you. Come on."

The other man was just behind Woods.

He could shout for help, but knew that wouldn't do any good, it would only postpone the inevitable, for these men were known and feared. He took refuge in words.

"What—what do you want me for? I don't know anything, I swear, if I did I wouldn't tell anybody!"

"If you know your way about you might even get paid for not telling anybody," Winn said, and now he seemed earnest, "We're not going to hurt you, Woody. We just want to get a few things straight, and there's a little job you can do for us at the plant. Don't argue. Come."

So Woods went with them.

But he was still afraid.

Chapter Eleven

Paint Trouble

Roger put thought of Woods and the two night-shift labourers out of his mind when Sheppard went out: the sergeant wouldn't miss much. He was anxious to see Michael Grannett again, but a word with Popham would be timely. A man who thought he was taken for granted always lost his enthusiasm and was more liable to error.

"Someone will have to persuade Sheppy to wear a wig," Roger said; "he can't do that conjuring trick with his hat all the time."

Popham found that a huge joke. "I'll have more thatch than him when I'm ninety!"

"I'll bet you will. Things all right with you?"

"As far as I know, sir. I'm card-indexing all messages and reports this way …"

Roger spent three minutes looking over the system and approving it, and then said: "That's fine. You've got special cards for Munro, Harrison, Amory, Teresa Lee – that's a good thought – Torrance, and Michael Grannett. Add that hospital Sister, Marsh, and young Woods, will you?"

"Yes, right away."

"Thanks. That stuff from the Yard should be here soon, but don't send for me unless there's something sensational." Roger went out, leaving Popham purring, and asked his way to the Paint Shop and the elder Grannett. 'Paint Shop' proved to be an almost ludicrous misnomer. It was another vast building, brightly lit, and the smell of paint and cellulose was overpowering to anyone not used to it. It was fascinating to see the car bodies on their never-ending conveyors, going into one long tunnel painted a dirty reddish brown, coming out at the other end bright and shiny apple-green, and then going into a second tunnel, which was obviously sealed, and at the side of which were some steps leading up to an opening marked: *Observation Platform*.

Grannett was standing by a small desk, with a lot of papers spread out in front of him. He glanced round at Roger, but didn't smile.

"'Morning."

"Good morning," said Roger, and lost no time. "Still think that Munro murdered your brother?"

"I do, and I always shall." Grannett looked wary, but there was less bitterness in his voice than there had been yesterday, and perhaps not the same hardness in his eyes. "And I expect you to prove it."

"What makes you harp on the word 'murder'?"

"Because that's what it was."

"Under law, if Munro started the fight it would be manslaughter; if he didn't, accidental death."

Grannett said: "I call it murder." He stared hard into Roger's eyes, and went on: "And whatever the police or the law call it, I shall always say that it was murder. My brother hadn't a chance."

"Did you know that it was being said that he was put up to pick this quarrel?"

"It's a damned lie."

"Sure?"

"All right, Mr Chief Inspector," Grannett said, with a scowl, "you're on the side of the directors. Who's surprised? Old Munro is married to the sister of a cabinet minister. He'll pull plenty of strings, and you'll dance to whatever strings he pulls."

"Now you listen to me," Roger said very quietly. "I want to find out the truth, and I'm not satisfied I've got it all yet. If I felt that it would be justified, I'd make a charge of manslaughter or even murder. Can you be absolutely positive that your brother wasn't paid to pick a quarrel with Munro?"

"Hell of a lot of time he had, hadn't he?"

"It was known that Munro usually reached the factory about that time, it was known he was due, so there's nothing odd about it. The quarrel could have been laid on beforehand. If it comes to that, you could have staged the meeting where you did to make sure that the crowd was in the car's way."

Grannett's eyes narrowed again, in a kind of tired hostility.

"So that's it. *I'm* supposed to have put my brother up to picking this quarrel. That's the way the Munros want it, and perhaps that's the way they'll get it, but it isn't true. Oh, I know what they'll say: that I knew Munro was a crazy hot-head, and if he ran into trouble he'd turn the workers against him, and that would strengthen my hand. I'm blamed for every item of trouble there's been at Munro Motors in the last five years, ever since I became chief shop steward. Well, as a matter of fact, Mr West, I've toned *down* a lot of claims on the management. There are plenty of Communists here who are spoiling for a strike all the time, and who want to make all the trouble they can between management and men. If I let them lead me by the nose we'd have more labour trouble at Munro's than anywhere else in the country. But what do we get? Far less than the average. You can't show me another car manufacturer with such a clean record. Doesn't it strike you as peculiar that while I've been the men's spokesman we've had so little trouble? Do you think that's all because of the management, or Mr Amory? Take it from me, it isn't. All I've ever asked for is a fair cut for the workers, and I've had a hell of a time getting it, but I've always got it. I always knew who was the chief obstacle. It wasn't Paul Munro, the one who died; he was reasonable enough. It wasn't Amory – if it hadn't been for him, the only director who could see the workers' point of view as well as the management's, we'd have had trouble all along the line. The real obstacle's been Sir Ian, and he'll have his own son on his side all right. That's why we've got to get this extra ten per cent now. If we don't, there'll be hell to pay later on."

"Why should there be?" Roger asked.

He was oblivious of the dozens of people nearby, many of them standing and looking on. His interest was only in Grannett; and he had to admit the reasonableness of Grannett's manner, and the logic of most of his arguments. His resentment of Sir Ian was as strong as ever, and obviously it spilled over on to Malcolm; but it wasn't the blind, fanatical hatred of a man of one class for another. It had been fed on bitterness.

"If you'd studied labour problems the way I have, you'd know without asking," Grannett answered at last. "Probably you don't know there *are* any problems. Let me tell you about some of them. We've got our share of Commies, as I've said. We've had our share of trouble because of high prices on the export market and Suez and a lot of other things. We know that if we're to hold our jobs, we've got to keep prices down, but you can't do that by keeping wages down, too. What you've got to do is raise wages high, and then get the production out of the workers. Handled the right way, they'll give it.

"But they're always being needled," Grannett went on, and he gave Roger a very firm impression: that he was really dedicated to his job. Every word seemed to prove that. "This time, they've done a damned good job on Mark 9. They've produced ten per cent more than was estimated, too. They've got them down to a price which can compete with German, Italian, and French cars, and beat most of them. Now the orders are streaming in. The factory will be working at full stretch for twelve months, simply on the strength of those orders, and it's making a fortune for the shareholders. So the men want a share of what's going, and they're going to get it. Don't give me the argument that they've got to produce the goods first and get the bonus afterwards, because it never works out that way. Something always comes along to make it impossible for the management to pay up. And if the men work for six months on the present standard wage, make a fortune for the shareholders, and *then* ask for their bonus, they'll run into Sir Ian and either a flat' no' or a small offer. Then they'll be really mad. Then the Commies will get at them. And *then* Munro's will really have strike trouble, and trouble I can't control. That's why I want the ten per cent now."

Roger said slowly, thoughtfully: "And you think Sir Ian stands in the way of it?"

"I know he does."

"And that's why you hate him?"

That surprised Grannett.

There was a pause, and then he said deliberately, looking Roger straight in the eyes: "That's why I hate what he does."

"And you think his son will be on his side?"

"I'm damned sure he will be. I know the type."

"And is that why you have set out to discredit Malcolm Munro?"

The question came almost gently, and at first Grannett didn't see its significance. When he did, he set his jaw tightly, and Roger thought that he would turn away.

A tall, thin man with a broken nose and wearing a paint-daubed overall came over, a little splay-footed, touched his forehead to Roger, and said to Grannett: "Ready to change over to red, Mike. How about it?"

"How many green have you done?" Grannett switched his thoughts on the instant.

"Two hundred."

"Do another hundred, will you, Lanky? " Grannett said. "There's been a new order, they phoned up ten minutes ago. How's the heat tunnel? "

"It's okay."

"We don't want any more of that blister trouble."

"We won't get it, it was just a mistake."

"It was a damned expensive mistake," Grannett said, and when the man had gone off he made an entry in a book on the desk, then turned to Roger and said unexpectedly: "I'm trying to save the firm money, but you wouldn't believe that, would you? I'm trying to make sure that we all get a good profit. I don't like waste any more than the Munros like it, and as far as I can, I make sure that we don't get it. That new heat tunnel cooks the cellulose," he added when he saw Roger staring at the doorway marked *Observation Platform*, through which the tall man disappeared. "The car bodies go through that spray tunnel, and then into the heat tunnel, where they're cooked, or heated, to make sure of even drying and resistance to all kinds of weather conditions. The last time we did apple-green, Lanky set the temperature too high, and we ruined fifty jobs before it was discovered. Like to know who got called down for that? I did. The Works Manager would have fired me if he'd had a bit more guts."

Roger said: "No one doubts your guts, but how about answering my question?"

"You're a copper," Grannett said, and now there was a faint smile at his lips, almost a sneer. "You have to ask questions. I think you're probably a good copper, too, and you'll do your best. I hope you get all the right answers while you're here, but you won't if you stay with the directors too long, and drink too much of their whisky. I didn't set out to discredit Malcolm Munro. I didn't have to. He did it all by himself."

"I hope I don't find out anything different," said Roger. "Do you know the men who attacked him last night?"

"No." Now, Grannett grinned more broadly. "And I didn't set them on to him, either."

"Did you know he was attacked at his house, just before you arrived with that ill-advised note?"

"Ill-advised, my foot," Grannett said jeeringly. "That letter will do Ian Munro more harm than anything else I can think of. It'll get him worried and make him unsure of himself – now his son's future's at stake, see? The old devil will bluster, but he'll be careful. I know what I'm doing."

"And you'll use your brother's death as a tool to make the Munros do what you want. Is that it?"

Grannett's smile faded into grimness, and he answered very softly: "Yes, if needs be, I'll do that. Listen, Mr West. There are over six thousand employees at this factory, and they've got about twenty thousand dependants, probably more. Old folk, sick folk, kids, babies, more babies on the way. Munro Motors are life and death to them. It's a lot of people to have to worry about, and I'll use anything I can get to win everything they need. Sentiment won't stop me. Let me tell you something else, too. When Munro killed my brother and sacked young Woods, he put the whole factory against him, and that also means against the board of directors. The fact that some young fools tried to beat him up doesn't alter the situation. I'm told that Woods has been reinstated, but the damage is done, don't make any mistake. When I say 'strike' the men will come out, and I'll say strike unless the Board gives us what we're asking for. Don't make any mistake about that, either. We've got the Board where we want them. They may not know it yet, but they soon will. Most of this has arisen because my kid brother was killed. I'd be smearing his memory if I didn't use his death the best way I could."

Roger obviously puzzled him by smiling as he finished, and then remarking: "Didn't I hear you call Sir Ian Munro ruthless?"

"That's the word," Grannett agreed, and broke off and moved away quickly. The door into the heat tunnel was open, and the lanky, splay-footed man came hurrying.

"What's up?" Grannett called, above the clanking of the metal and the whirr of the machines. "Don't tell me that blasted oven's too hot again."

"It's a bit high already," the lanky man said. "If you ask me, there's something wrong with the thermostat. We ought to stop work until the electricians have had a go at it."

"Or maybe you forgot to turn a switch," Grannett growled. "I'll have a look myself." He strode to the observation platform, and Roger followed, saw him climbing up into a small platform built into the tunnel. Beyond him was the interior of the heat tunnel. Roger saw the apple-green cars hanging nose downwards, and passing one after the other. Grannett pulled a switch and the conveyor belt stopped. He examined some other switches, then went down into the shop again, Roger with him. "I think you're right, Lanky," he said. "I'll ask Colonel Harrison to bring the chief electrician along."

"So long as you don't blame me," Lanky said gloomily.

"We won't, if it's not your fault."

"Want me to turn off the heat?"

"Not yet," Grannett said. "Not until they've been to see it." He went back to the desk, ignoring Roger, lifted a telephone and asked for the Works Manager. Then he said: "It's Grannett speaking. There's something wrong with the heat tunnel, ask him if he'll come along with Mr Willson, will you? Yes, quick." He rang off, pushed his fingers through that wiry red hair, and looked sombrely at Roger. "I'm going to have my hands full for the rest of the day, this is one of the worst bottlenecks in production. If you've got anything else to ask, you'd better make it snappy."

Roger said: "Thanks. How long had your brother been friendly with Hugh Torrance?"

"Friendly isn't the word I'd use," said Grannett promptly. "He hero-worshipped him. I tried to stop it, because one of these days Torrance was going to break his neck, but the kid was fascinated by speed. If I knew what I know now, perhaps I'd have encouraged him to have his fun while he could." Grannett paused, then widened his eyes, and actually grinned crookedly. "You get around, don't you? And you persuade people to talk more than they want to. So you think that Torrance hated Munro's guts because of the girl, and maybe he put Roy up to quarrelling with Munro? That's two theories you've advanced, Mr West. You'd better take your choice."

He looked towards the main entrance to the shop, and his expression changed swiftly, becoming granite hard: Roger did not think he had ever seen such bleakness in a man's eyes, and turned to see why.

Sir Ian, Colonel Harrison, and Amory were coming along the side of the motionless conveyor belt.

Roger waited.

Sir Ian nodded brusquely. Amory was not his usual smiling self, and gave the impression that he was keenly aware of the possibilities of an open clash between the shop steward and the Chairman.

It was Harrison who said with an accusing sharpness in his voice: "Why has the belt stopped, Grannett? Haven't we had enough trouble here already? "

Roger thought: 'I don't know what good Harrison is, but either he wants to goad Grannett into losing his temper or he's a complete fool.'

Chapter Twelve

Rumour on Wings

Grannett maintained his composure surprisingly well; almost too well. One would expect him to be more edgy than usual after the shock of his brother's death, but he seemed to be able to shake it off. It was easy to remember that he intended to use the tragedy cold-bloodedly, so as to get his way over the wage claim.

"It was getting too hot again," he said. "The control man's been watching it specially, since the trouble last week. He had the right switches down and the right temperature control, but it was getting too hot. I checked. Then I stopped the belt, because I thought we'd better lose some production than risk a lot more spoiled jobs and possible complaints from customers."

Harrison grunted.

Amory was perhaps a little over-anxious to conciliate.

"Very wise, and the quicker we find out the cause of the trouble, the better," he soothed.

"I'll see you in the office," Sir Ian said, and nodded again to Roger and walked on. Grannett behaved as if he didn't exist, and walked with Harrison and Amory to the door at the side of the tunnel. Roger heard them talking, knew after five minutes that they had decided to turn the heat off, let the tunnel cool down, and then find out what was wrong with the heating units. He gathered that these had to be inspected from inside the tunnel, but the technical terms used were too unfamiliar for him to know exactly what they meant.

Another man came up, short, freckly, earnest. Harrison greeted him as Willson, so this was the electrician.

"… how soon can you get it started?" Amory asked.

"We'll cool it down in ten minutes, should be able to see what's what then," answered Willson. He was not quite Cockney. "I won't take a minute longer than I can help, I promise that."

"Sure you won't," Amory said. "George—" That was to Harrison. "Will you stay here until Willson's got the unit down, and let me know how bad it is?"

"Yes." Harrison's nod was like a salute.

"Thanks," said Amory, and turned to Roger, smiled apologetically, and went on: "I wonder if you can spare me half an hour, Chief Inspector?"

"Yes, of course," Roger said. "Right away?"

"Please."

The others were at the observation platform, and Roger walked briskly along with Amory, and in the wake of Sir Ian. Amory didn't speak until they were out of the Paint Shop. The fresh air smelt particularly good, quickly relieving Roger's slight feeling of nausea from the cellulose.

Sir Ian Munro, just outside, looked very sturdy, very lonely, and somehow, Roger thought, a little pathetic.

Beyond him was a tall, new-looking building with two squat chimneys; it had the look of a power station, and was exactly that: the station which supplied all the power to the plant, which had much more automation in than most. Roger had seen it several times before, but had not been so close as he was now.

"They'll telephone us about the heat tunnel," Amory said. "I shouldn't think it's serious."

"It's not only serious," Sir Ian asserted, in a growling voice, "it's deliberate. We're going to have hold-up after hold-up in production. It's a form of blackmail. How far is that a crime, Chief Inspector? How far is it a crime wilfully to obstruct the nation's economy? Isn't it a form of sabotage?"

"Can it be proved?" asked Roger mildly.

"Proved," echoed Sir Ian, in a hopeless bark, "how can it be? Whispers here, whispers there. A movement of a switch. The breaking of a fuse through deliberate overloading. Mixing wrong colours. Time and time and time again we have trouble due to sabotage, but proof—"

He broke off abruptly, stared straight ahead of him, then took out a fat gold cigarette case and proffered it. "I haven't thanked you sufficiently for saving my son's life last night, Mr West. I don't suppose I can ever thank you enough. And I'm grateful that you've taken the precaution of having him escorted wherever he goes. I would like to ask a favour of you."

That must have cost him something to say.

"Yes, sir," Roger said. He had to be patient, remember to subordinate himself to these people, even appear humble. And he had to watch every step he made and weigh every word that these men said.

They all lit cigarettes from Amory's lighter.

"My son will soon resent being watched at home and followed wherever he goes," Sir Ian declared. "He will see it as an insult to his courage and ability to take care of himself. While there remains the slightest danger, I hope you will continue to take the precautions that you're taking now."

"Be sure of it," Roger promised.

"Thank you."

"Apart from what happened yesterday, do you know of any reason why he should be in danger?" Roger asked.

"Do I?" Sir Ian looked at Amory. No one else was in earshot, and the sun was warm upon them. "Well, Bob, do I?"

"I don't think we'll gain anything by withholding facts from the police," Amory said, sounding more at ease, as if he felt that a crisis was past.

"No, we won't. Chief Inspector," Sir Ian went on portentously, "our chief test driver has become somewhat erratic and unreliable of late. We have reason to believe that it is because he considers that my son has stolen his young woman. My son and Torrance were once close friends. I'm not saying I think that Torrance knows anything about these attacks, but he has both shown and expressed enmity towards my son. That is what Mr Amory thought you should be told."

It would be easy to say: 'Yes, I know all about that,' but it wouldn't do any good. Sir Ian had obviously made a great effort to unbend so far; and this was probably why Amory had wanted to talk, why Amory, the reasonable man, the mediator, the peacemaker, was so much more at ease.

"I take it that you know of no other possible reason?" Roger asked.

"None whatsoever."

"Thank you again, sir," Roger said, and expected the others to go, but Sir Ian spoke again, abruptly.

"I don't know what Grannett was saying to you, Mr West. I know he's a smooth-tongued scoundrel, and can talk himself out of any trouble. He fools a lot of people, but he doesn't fool me, and I hope you won't let him fool you. I know this factory in every aspect, Mr West. I know every job, in every department. I helped to build Munro Motors with my own hands. In the early days – within twenty yards of the spot where we are standing now, where that little summer-house is, I helped to make the first prototype of the old Munro Marvel. I have followed every development since, driven the prototype of every model – even Mark 9. Until automation came there was not a job in this whole plant that I could not do if the need arose. I knew everything. Mr Amory here is our automation specialist, but I'm sufficiently familiar with what goes on to know that we have more mechanical trouble with Grannett's department than anywhere else, and I don't believe that is just coincidence."

"While I'm here," Roger said, not asserting himself at all, "I may be able to find out."

"I hope you will," Sir Ian said gruffly, and then Amory spoke; Roger realised that the managing director hadn't yet explained the reason for his request for 'half an hour'. His gaze was very straight, and it was easy to believe that he would be as blunt as Sir Ian.

"May I ask exactly what you're looking for now, Mr West? Surely you have made all the inquiries you need to make about the accident." When Roger didn't answer, Amory went on: "Is it true that you believe that young Grannett was in fact murdered?"

So the truth had leaked out, and there would be little point in denying it There might be some in trying to make sure that it wasn't spread any farther. Roger felt the anxious gaze of both men on him, as well as the warmth of the sun, as he said: "There are reasons for wondering whether we yet know the real cause of death, gentlemen, and until we can be positive, I want to stay here. Ostensibly I'm still trying to find out who attacked your son and exactly what happened yesterday lunchtime. I hope I can rely on you not to spread any different rumours."

"Last thing we'd want to do," said Sir Ian.

"You'll probably wonder what prompted my question," said Amory. "It's very simply this: the Sister reported a surprising deterioration in the youth's condition between the time he was received at the factory hospital and the time he left. She couldn't account for it, and told me so. And I understand that the police have been inquiring closely into the movements of everyone who went to the hospital. Is that right? "

"Yes."

"Did you know that I was there?"

"You, Mr Malcolm, Mr Torrance, Michael Grannett, Colonel Harrison, Sister Marsh of course, and possibly several others," Roger answered. "I think I can assure you that we won't leave anything undone."

"I'm quite sure you won't," Amory said grimly. "I want to say again that anything and everything we can do to help clear up the mystery is at your service."

"Thank you, sir."

"And I know you realise that if it can be cleared up quickly it might make all the difference at the factory," Amory went on. "The difference between a strike and no strike. The difference between plenty for all the workers and their dependants for years and a very hard time. At the moment the workers are in an extremely stubborn mood."

Sir Ian nearly exploded. "Stubborn? They're mulish! Rather than put their rate up, I'd let them stay on strike for the rest of the year. And if they won't accept our terms, I'd make it a lockout into the bargain."

Amory became sharp. "I hope you won't repeat what you've just heard, Mr West."

"I won't," Roger promised, and watched Sir Ian striding off and Amory hurrying to catch him up.

He wondered where they'd heard the talk of murder, and whether Malcolm had heard it yet.

Tessa watched as Malcolm walked from the Rolls-Bentley to the office building, head high, face set, looking as if he knew that everyone was watching him, and that he didn't care a damn. She now knew that he cared a great deal. It was odd that with so many worries and such fear for him, her heart could be light as she watched him, and she could feel a kind of happiness. He glanced up at her, and she expected his sternness to fade, a swift flash of a smile to replace it.

He looked straight at her; but didn't smile.

She felt suddenly helplessly unhappy.

"You're just a sentimental *fool,*" she told herself savagely, and tears stung her eyes. "It was bound to happen."

She felt so sure what had caused his aloofness.

Robert Amory had heard her "Malcolm, darling!" and Sir Ian had seen them together. She wasn't in their class. Sir Ian would be very conscious of it, would bring great pressure to bear to make Malcolm see the folly of it.

She banged at her typewriter, but kept pausing, to listen for him. He would go into his office by the passage door, of course, not this one.

Her door opened, and he came in. For a moment, she sat with fingers poised over the keys, not turning her head. It had hurt so much; even a hint of a smile, a nod, a wave would have helped.

He said stonily: "So you've heard, too."

"Heard?" That made her look round. The plaster, the bruises, and the scratches made him look almost comical, but his eyes made him look frightening. "Heard what?"

"For God's sake, must *we* fence?"

"I don't know what you're talking about."

"You just preferred looking at the typewriter when I came in, is that it? A bandaged beauty doesn't appeal to you."

"Malcolm, please!" This was absurd; he was bitter for no reason at all. "If you—"

She broke off, as he drew nearer.

"If I what?"

"If you'd—oh, it seems so ridiculous." And it did. "If you'd smiled at me as you passed outside, instead of looking as if I didn't exist, I'd be less interested in the typewriter."

His expression changed a little, and he drew nearer still.

"Just now?"

"Yes."

"I didn't see you."

"But you looked!"

"The sun was reflected on the window. I couldn't see in."

She said helplessly: "Oh, what a fool. I thought you didn't want—"

"If you thought I'd ever pass you without a nod or a wink you certainly were a fool." His hands were firm on her shoulders, and she felt his tension, sensed his desire. But he did not kiss her. "Tessa, I love you. I measure everything else against that." He pressed more heavily on her shoulders. "Understand?"

"Yes. Yes, darling. And I—" She felt so weak, so humble.

"Don't say you love me," Malcolm interrupted. "Not until after you've heard the latest news, anyhow. Roy Grannett was murdered."

She heard, but it didn't really sink in.

"Murdered, get it?" he repeated. "And I am the obvious number one suspect. Roy Grannett was cold-bloodedly murdered, and I face an enemy on each side. The police, with a nice murder charge up their sleeve, and the factory."

"Darling, don't joke about it! The police couldn't possibly suspect you."

"Don't be fooled by West's nice manner and sweet smile," Malcolm warned. "That man is the most efficient policeman in the country. Look." He moved his hands, and went to the window, and Tessa stood up to see what he was pointing at, "That big chap is my shadow. Wherever I go I'm watched."

"But that's to protect you," she asserted.

"To protect me from the others who seem to want me dead," Malcolm said, and then suddenly he turned and looked at her, and took her cool hands. There was a fierce yet helpless look in his eyes. "That business outside last night and the near shave this morning really shook me, Tess. I'm scared."

"You needn't be." She tried to reassure him. "There's no need at all, you needn't be."

But she knew that she would be, also, until they had learned the truth.

Later, when she was alone, she wondered almost guiltily:

'*Do* the police suspect him?'

Angrily, she said no.

But if they did, why should they?

Chapter Thirteen

Death By Remote Control

Roger walked briskly away from the old summer-house, which was so obviously kept there for sentimental reasons, and approached the Assembly Shop. He felt that he was making as much progress with the management as he could expect; possibly more. Even Sir Ian would consider anything he suggested, it wasn't just talk that he would be given every facility.

He went back to his office in the Assembly Shop, to be greeted by Popham with the news that Torrance had a fractured femur, and was badly bruised everywhere, but was not on the danger list. He would be off duty for months.

Knightley had telephoned from the Yard, to say that the pathologist's report was fully accepted; there was no lingering doubt that Roy Grannett had been murdered.

Then the dossiers arrived. Most were disappointing, serving only to confirm everything that the police already knew, but one startled him.

Colonel Harrison had a nervous breakdown in 1950, and spent three years in a private asylum.

'Did he, then,' Roger reflected, and the Colonel's face, so white and with an expression almost of vacancy, seemed to appear in his mind's eye. The military type, the man who seemed to act by reflexes. This was a thing to remember.

No new names were added to the list of those known to have been in the factory hospital the previous afternoon. The vital factor was the timing, and that wasn't easy to establish with absolute accuracy. No formal record was kept, and the factory hospital doors were open to all and sundry. There was nothing like the formality of an ordinary hospital. Once he began to inquire too closely the truth about the murder would spread.

He checked the timing as far as he could.

His telephone bell rang, and he said: "West here," as if he was at his own office, and was startled to hear Charley Coombs speak in a voice both agitated and excited.

"Handsome, I've really got something for you this time. I've found a weapon."

"What kind of weapon?"

"Come off it! Our old pal, the blunt instrument," said Coombs, and there was no doubt about his excitement. "I've been talking to Sister Marsh, and she's sure the kid wasn't at death's door when she first saw him. But if someone hit young Grannett when he was lying on the couch at the hospital, we'd be on the way."

"Any idea who did it?" Roger demanded.

"Goddammit, not over the telephone," Charley squealed. "Forgotten you're not at the Yard, Handsome? Can you come and meet me right away?"

"You bet I can. Where?"

"Know the Chassis Shop?"

"Not really well."

"Anyone will tell you," said Coombs. "Buck up, Handsome! I don't want to leave this spot, there might be something useful to pick up. Come out of the main entrance and turn right, then ask anyone. I'm at the finishing end of Conveyor 3."

"Right." Roger felt the kind of excitement that he knew Coombs must feel. Coombs had been away from the Yard a long time, but obviously all the old familiar sensations were back in him; the thrill of the chase, the exhilaration of a discovery which might help to trap a killer, all the things which were the breath of life to Roger now, and had been to Coombs a few years ago. Roger hurried, still watched; here and there people waved to him. He wondered whether they had fooled him; how many of them knew the real manner of young Grannett's death? That Sister might have talked freely too, so that the word 'murder' would soon be spread over the whole of the factory.

A hooter was blowing as he left the main doors; the lunchtime signal for some of the shift. He asked a little wizened woman in a khaki overall where the Chassis Shop was, and she pointed, told him, and stood gaping after him. It was another huge shed like the Assembly Shop, and also painted dark-green. A stream of people were coming away, and several stood aside to let Roger pass; he had only been in here once before, but everyone recognised him. Then he heard the crash inside: a terrifying sound.

Charley Coombs was thoroughly enjoying himself.

He had been a good man at the Yard for thirty years, and had retired at sixty with a Chief Inspector's pension, but had been too restless to settle down to home and garden. So he had found this job. It wasn't exactly what he liked. He had a staff of a dozen men, all ex-policemen, whose chief job was to check all goods and prevent all kinds of pilfering and petty crimes. Thanks to Charley, there was comparatively little.

To be back on a real investigation was like being home.

Now, he had some evidence which would shake West.

Charley chuckled to himself as he stood by the Number 3 conveyor, holding a hammer wrapped inside a newspaper underneath his coat and lodged at his waistband so that no one else could see it. The marks of blood, and the several red hairs sticking to the smooth head, were too much for coincidence, and he believed he knew who had put it where he had found it – under a pile of old metal scraps just outside the shop. Obviously it had been pushed underneath with a foot, and some of the scrap metal pulled over it. There might be a print on the hammer, even though it had been wiped, possibly this was enough to prove the theory that he was bursting to pass on to Handsome West.

The factory hooter went.

Charley Coombs had forgotten that he was hungry; now he remembered. It wouldn't be the first time he had missed a meal in the cause of justice, and he actually chuckled at what he believed would be West's astonishment when he told his tale.

He glanced up.

The Chassis Shop was a little different from the others, but a conveyor system was in operation here too. There were two operations: one, that of fitting on the wheels, which was done by men on a platform while a chassis was on the upper conveyor; two, putting in the engine, done when the cars were lowered and the belt stopped for just long enough for the job to be done. It took only minutes. Somewhere else in this huge 'shop' were other conveyors where men did various jobs. The chassis, looking like burnished skeletons, passed a foot or so above Charley's head at this point. No men worked just here – it was the spot where repair and maintenance jobs were done, and where a faulty chassis could be lowered and taken off the conveyor.

A chassis above him was rattling, but the noise was so familiar that he didn't give it a second thought, except to glance up.

In sudden, awful horror, he saw it falling. He did not have a chance to dodge. The chassis weighed over a ton, and a hub struck Charley squarely on the head. He did not hear the hideous crash.

Roger stared grimly down at the ex-Yard man, who had been flung to one side and who lay so still. A lot was happening already.

A crowd had gathered, and First Aid men were already on the way, but no one could glance at Charley and think there was a gleam of hope. The only good thing was that death had been quick.

Good?

In Roger's hands was the newspaper containing the hammer. He had found this, and seen at a glance why Charley had been so excited. Once it was proved that those red hairs belonged to dead Roy Grannett, this could be identified as the murder weapon.

Roger's jaws were set tightly; painfully.

He heard the words 'awful accident'.

It was no more an accident than young Grannett's death, or the attacks on Malcolm Munro. Someone had made that chassis fall deliberately. He didn't know how the operations worked, but was quite sure that there was a way of controlling the chassis from a control panel; a form of remote control, as in the Assembly Shop.

It should be easy enough to find out who had had access to it five minutes ago.

He saw Harrison, stocky, grey, outwardly calm, hurrying with military precision towards the spot. So Harrison must have been in this part of the plant when the chassis had fallen.

Harrison saw Charley, and blanched. He looked nearer human than he had at any time. He stared down, lips parted, then gulped and looked up at Roger.

He muttered: "Ghastly."

Roger said in a hard voice: "I want to see the control panel, and I want to see it quick. I've had the shop doors shut, and I've asked for a loudspeaker announcement that no one must leave the shop for the next half hour. Not until I've given permission. Confirm it, please."

"But—but what good will that do?" Harrison, stammered.

"It might keep in the man who touched the control for this chassis."

"Surely—such an accident might happen anywhere."

"Let's get that announcement confirmed," Roger said. "Do you have a loudspeaker control in the shop office?"

"Yes. Yes, I—" Harrison moistened his lips again. "It's unbelievable." He glanced at Coombs and his crushed head, and at the wrecked and twisted chassis. The First Aid men arrived; even they stopped short when they saw what had happened. "Come along," Harrison managed to say. "Dreadful. Dreadful to have happened just now." He looked as though he would faint

"What difference does the timing make?" Roger could have struck him, was in a savage enough mood to strike anybody, to throw all his careful humouring of these men to the winds.

"We were having a tour of inspection," Harrison muttered. "All of us. With—with some clients from overseas."

Roger didn't comment.

A group of men stood by the glass walls of the office in this shop. Roger recognised the two Americans, the Swede, and three members of Munro's board. Everyone on the other suspect list was here except Mike Grannett, and Grannett would have fellow shop stewards, probably many friends, everywhere in the plant.

"We—we were examining the control panel. One—one of us must have touched it by accident," Harrison muttered. "Each—each chassis is separately controlled. The release button should not be pressed until the chassis has been lowered." He seemed to need words to help him. "Oh, God, this is ghastly, ghastly."

The others were approaching, slowly. Fearfully?

Roger went to meet them.

As they met, the clatter and the rattling, the hum of machines and the clatter of footsteps stopped, and as they stopped, men ceased to talk and there was strange silence everywhere.

Chapter Fourteen

One Man Out?

It was Amory who spoke, while Sir Ian opened his mouth, closed it again, then set his lips tightly, as if he did not intend to allow a word to escape.

"We are most dreadfully sorry about this," Amory said. "Is it true that it was ex-Inspector Coombs?"

"Yes." Roger spoke like a different, ruthless man. The shock of Coombs' death laid an icy hand upon him. Once he had absorbed it, he might see much that had been hidden before. His first job was to try to make sure who had caused Coombs' death. But he must still watch his step, must not put a foot wrong avoidably. "I understand that all of you were at the control panel when it happened," he went on.

"That is so."

"I'd like you all to come back to it with me," Roger said. He did not appear to glance at the two Americans and the Swede, two tall and one short man, all immaculately dressed, but he saw their expressions.

Bewildered?

The taller of the Americans said: "We would like to associate ourselves with Mr Amory's sentiments, we are very sorry, very sorry indeed."

"Terribly sorry," the other emphasised.

"Most regrettable," said the Swede.

"Gentlemen, will you please go back to the directors' room?" Amory said. "We will come just as soon as we can."

"I'd like everyone to come with me," Roger said. "No exceptions, please."

Amory looked surprised, Sir Ian opened his mouth again, but swallowed comment; perhaps Amory had made him realise that he had talked too much already.

"Surely that isn't necessary?" Amory could also be sharp.

"Essential," Roger said. "Don't let's waste time."

He felt a desperate need of urgency; seconds might count. Coombs had made his discovery only a few minutes ago, and in those few minutes his death had been plotted and murder carried out. It was uncanny speed, and in that speed must lie part of the answer to all the problems. Find who had made that chassis fall, and the case would break. He must be as fast as the killers.

Behind Malcolm Munro and the others was Tessa Lee. Roger was surprised to see her, but as she was secretary to the sales director, it wasn't really surprising. She led the way, with Malcolm a step behind her. A silent company of workers stood watching, strangely like mourners. The only sounds came from the corner where Coombs lay dead, and these were hushed, and would not have been heard had the conveyors been working.

The party reached the offices, which were like those in the Assembly Shop, with glass walls round the outside, and frosted glass keeping the managerial staff out of sight of the factory itself. Here were time-clocks and racks of time-cards, a dozen clerks working or staring around. A short, brisk-looking man in his shirtsleeves came up.

"How long will we have to keep the belts still?" he asked Amory.

Amory looked at Roger.

"I don't want to interfere with more than I must," Roger said, "but we'll have to make an exhaustive examination of the chassis which fell, and of the conveyor hooks from which it fell. We'll also need to examine that section of the control panel which controls Conveyor 3." He tried to hide his surging impatience.

The short man said as if outraged: "But that's impossible! We'd have to stand a couple of hundred workers off for the rest of the day, and we're desperately short of chassis." He appealed to Amory, as to an oracle.

"If you'd like to consult my superiors, please do, but don't waste any time," Roger said. "I have to telephone them at once, anyway."

"I'll let you know in ten minutes or so," Amory promised the short man. "Keep everything at a standstill. Better give the working shift its break now. The canteens can cope, and that might see us through."

"Very good idea, sir." The short man looked almost malevolently at Roger.

"I will give the order," Harrison said.

"You won't forget that no one is to leave the shed until I've given the word, will you?" Roger asked crisply.

He felt the resentment of everyone present, but wasn't sure how deep it went. Those earlier efforts to win their co-operation might come in useful now, or might prove to have been a waste of time. Certainly the smooth flow of production meant much more to them than the life or death of Charley Coombs. But no one argued any more. Harrison stamped ahead, and before the others reached the office his voice came over loudspeakers placed all about the great shed. It seemed very loud, because of the unaccustomed stillness.

Then they all reached the office. The short man, presumably the Shop Manager, led the way along the glass-walled passages and up a short flight of steps to the big central room, rather like a control room at Scotland Yard, but with much larger panels, each with dozens of finger pushes, each with many red lights glowing. This was higher than the rest of the offices, and glass walls ensured a clear view of the vast shop. The panels faced the end where Coombs had been struck down, and the easily identifiable figure of Coombs must have been clearly visible from here.

Roger saw that there was one panel for each conveyor, there would be no difficulty in identifying Number 3. Harrison was standing at the side of the loudspeaker unit. Three control-board operators were standing by, all in their shirtsleeves; youngish, lean-faced men.

"Get some chairs," Harrison ordered abruptly.

The three men moved at once, and now everyone who could have touched that control button was here; the murderer was present, impassive of face, but probably desperate with fear.

Roger picked up a telephone.

"Give me the Scotland Yard officer in the Assembly Shop, please … Hallo, Popham? Is Sheppard there? … Good, put him on … Sergeant, there has been a fatality in the Chassis Shop, involving Mr Coombs … Yes, Coombs." He heard the horror in Sheppard's voice. "I want you to postpone the other job, and come to me at the Chassis Shop office at once. Have Popham bring in Tilbury and Marino to stand by … yes, leave the visit to Woods and the other pair … Right, thanks." He rang off, and saw the three control operators bringing in small chairs. He lifted the receiver again, said: "Whitehall 1212, please," and looked round at Amory: "Would you like to speak to Superintendent Knightley yourself?"

"You talk to him first," Amory said.

"Thanks."

"This is Scotland Yard …"

"Mr Knightley, please, West here." There was only a brief pause. "Hallo, sir. We've had more trouble."

"What kind of trouble?" Knightley demanded sharply.

It took Roger four minutes to explain tersely, another minute for Knightley to promise to send experts at once, and to say: "Handle it exactly as you think it needs, Handsome. If anyone there raises any objection, refer them to the Assistant Commissioner. Whoever touched that control button's right under your nose. Get him."

"I will. Thanks." Roger rang off, and said to the others, most of whom were now sitting down: "A senior officer and technical experts will be here soon, gentlemen, but I am to proceed with the inquiry forthwith. Directly the experts arrive, they will decide how soon work can be resumed. I'm sure I can rely on your co-operation. Were all of you present in the control room when the chassis fell?"

Malcolm said immediately: "Miss Lee wasn't. She came with a message just after the accident."

"Thank you. But I'd like her to stay here for the time being." Roger looked at the girl, with her face of such classic beauty ringed with dark hair; she seemed to have recovered from last night, and looked very fresh. Malcolm was holding her arm, protectively.

No one had protected Charley Coombs.

"Now I'd like each one of you to take up the exact position he was in at the time of the accident," Roger said. "Can you be sure at precisely what time it happened?"

An operator said: "Dead sure. We had a warning flash the minute the chassis came off. It was one-thirty-one, sir, just after the B section lunch signal had finished. See this model conveyor system, sir." He pointed to a miniature of the whole Chassis Shop, and went on: "If anything mechanical goes wrong a red light flashes here, and makes an automatic time recording there, sir. So we know the moment there's trouble, and can stop it from getting worse."

"Thanks," Roger said. He heard footsteps outside, and he looked round to see Sheppard coming. At the doorway Sheppard wore his hat; as he stepped inside he took it off, and the bright light glistened pinkly on his pate. "Sergeant, I want you to draw a diagram which will show exactly where each of the gentlemen present was standing when the chassis fell."

"Yes, sir." Sheppard took out a notebook and pencil.

"Tell you what," said Harrison unexpectedly. "We have some blueprints of the control room. One be helpful?"

"Very, sir, thank you."

The blueprint was soon stretched out and pinned down on to a desk, and the party was shuffling from one place to another. Roger let them sweat, and said to Sheppard: "Check all the push buttons for prints, Sergeant."

Sheppard did the simple thing, and breathed on the plastic press buttons, then peered at them; but the tip of a finger, even a fingernail, would give sufficient pressure. Sheppard soon looked up, and shook his head.

By then, the others were in position. Young Munro was farthest away from Number 3 panel; it looked as if Munro must have been out of reach of the deadly press-button. The girl was near him, now.

So were two of the operators, who had been at other panels. But the main group, Amory, Sir Ian Harrison, and the men from overseas were all clustered round the operator at Number 3. One of the Americans was saying in an infuriatingly relaxed voice: "Were you in front of me, Sam, or was I in front of you?"

"I was in front of you," said the man named Sam.

"I was exactly here." The Swede was at one side, and was not near enough to touch the board without stretching; almost certainly this had been done surreptitiously. Only those who knew how to handle the controls were likely to be involved; Roger wanted the overseas men as witnesses rather than as suspects.

From here anyone could see all over the shop; could see the fallen chassis and the spot where Coombs had been. The First Aid men had gone now, but others were there; probably including a doctor. Divisional CID men should be there soon, to take photographs, draw diagrams as Sheppard was now doing, questioning everyone who had been near.

Not one of the people present showed any sign of panic or alarm, the guilty one concealed his guilt with remarkable self-control; but no one else could have touched that press-button. The man who had killed Coombs was here, remember; a man who had acted with bewildering speed, learning of danger from Coombs and snatching at the opportunity to silence him.

That speed held a secret.

But minutes were flying, and no one seemed to be suffering from particular strain; they accepted the silence Roger forced on them.

Sir Ian spoke at last; abruptly.

"How long are you going to keep us here like a lot of stuffed dummies?"

"Not a moment longer than I must," Roger said. "You haven't forgotten that someone here touched the press-button which killed Coombs, have you?" Sir Ian didn't speak; no one showed any reaction, although Tessa Lee and Malcolm seemed to grip hands more tightly. "I am now going to ask each one in turn if he is satisfied that he is in the same spot as he was when the chassis dropped and the alarm signal showed," Roger went on, "and also if he is satisfied that his neighbours are in the same position."

"Goddammit, man!" Sir Ian exploded. "Anyone would think we were under suspicion!"

"Someone in this room touched that button, so someone in this room killed ex-Inspector Coombs," Roger said coldly. "I am only interested in finding out who it was and why it was done. That is the official police attitude, sir."

Amory's hand rested on Sir Ian's shoulder, as if placatingly. The American named Sam said: "Well, I have to congratulate you on the way you set about the problem, Chief Inspector."

"Thanks," said Roger, and watched Sheppard making circles on the blueprint, then writing in the names of the people standing on the spots represented by those circles. Harrison, Sir Ian, and the operator had been handiest to the panel, and Malcolm Munro, Amory, and the two Americans could have reached it by stretching.

Sheppard said: "I've finished, sir."

"Thanks. Now, operator," Roger went on, "exactly how much pressure is needed to release a chassis?"

"Just a touch of the finger, sir," the operator of Conveyor 3 said.

"No real pressure?"

"No, sir. Placing the finger in the right position is what matters, so as to make contact. The whole panel is power-operated."

"Did you touch any button during the inspection?"

"No, sir."

"Did you see anyone who did?"

"No, sir." The operator looked uneasy, for Sir Ian was glaring at him, as if waiting for him to say the wrong thing.

"If anyone touched a button he would have been seen," Amory pointed out.

"Unless there was a distraction," Roger said.

"As a matter of fact, sir, there was," asserted the operator eagerly. "The telephone rang, and in turning round towards it, I bumped into one of our guests, sir – trod on his toe, in fact." The man's eyes were glowing. "Everyone moved away a bit."

"I recall that distinctly," Harrison said.

"It was my toe," declared one of the Americans dryly.

"Thank you," Roger said, and looked at Amory. He longed for someone to show even the slightest sign of cracking. "Now I would like to have the full use of the nearest office, please, to interview each of you in turn. You'll understand that after each interview I must make sure that you cannot communicate with anyone who has not been questioned."

"No! I won't have it!" Sir Ian exploded. "This is an insult to my guests."

"Don't worry at all, Sir Ian, it's okay with us," said the American named Sam.

"I fully accept the officer's request," said the Swede, with a stiff bow.

"Thank you, gentlemen," Roger said. "It won't take long."

The questioning took him forty-five minutes. At the end of it he still did not know who had touched the fatal button.

"I've never seen such a lot of poker-faces," Sheppard said, when they were alone in the office in the Chassis Shop. "It was like a conspiracy. We ought to reduce the possibles down to those who were in the hospital yesterday afternoon and in the control room today. Torrance is out, for one."

"Not altogether." Roger had forced away the depression which had followed the absolute failure. "There could be collusion. But it looks as if someone in that control room knew that Coombs had made a damning discovery, and seized the chance to try to kill him. I wish to God Charley hadn't been so cautious over the telephone." He was silent for a moment, and then went on in an easier voice: "Then we need the Divisional chaps and everyone we've got to spare to find out what Charley'd been doing."

"I can tell you this much," said Sheppard. "As he was looking for something beneath a pile of scrap iron just outside, the guided tour party passed him. I got that from a chap as I came into the shop. Charley must have picked up something pretty hot. I expect it was the hammer."

"The killer didn't lose a moment, and Roy Grannett's killer acted pretty fast, too." The question of speed still nagged at Roger, but he changed the subject. "Send for a snack from the canteen, will you? We'll have a bite and get everything shipshape before the others come from the Yard. The quicker we can get that shop working, the better, and I'm not thinking of the directors, either." For the first time since he had found it, Roger took the hammer out of the newspaper and spread the paper out on the desk. "We want a quick test for prints on the handle, then a lab test on the head for the hair and blood groups. Send it to the Yard by special messenger."

"Right."

Roger went to the corner, where the chassis lay on its side. The two detective officers and Green of the Division were there, taking measurements, doing all the routine work.

Green seemed involved, and not ready to talk: probably he was badly upset, too. All who had known Charley Coombs had liked him.

Outside, the workers were standing about in small groups, idle, aimless; as they would be if the strike came. A larger group, farther away, was gathered about a man standing on a box and shouting: "I tell you we're being made fools of by the management. We ought to be out *now*, we never ought to have agreed to wait. Ten per cent is little enough, and if we workers stand together we'll get our rights."

Suddenly it became clear that Grannett knew exactly what he was talking about.

Then the experts arrived from the Yard, and within half an hour gave permission for all but Number 3 conveyor to be started up. Groups of men and women who had been standing about idly, many outside the shop, drifted into work again.

Roger had the heap of scrap metal, mostly bright and glistening, cordoned off, but dozens of people regularly put pieces on or took pieces off it; he wasn't likely to find out much from that – except that a killer had put the hammer there, and had seen Charley Coombs retrieve it.

Within another hour, Knightley telephoned from the Yard. The hairs on the hammer were identical with hairs taken from Roy Grannett's head, and the blood was of the same group; so that hammer had been used to kill the boy.

"All but a smear or so of prints were wiped off," Knightley said. "Not much hope of results from that. I'm sending the hammer back, for you to try to trace the owner. I'm also sending another three men, you'll probably need them. And listen, Handsome – start treating Munro's rough. I've just come from the A.C. and he agrees. If Sir Ian Munro starts to throw his weight about, tell him where he gets off. Same with the others. We'll back you to the hilt."

"That's fine." Roger felt a quick warmth of appreciation. "I won't rub any one up the wrong way for the sake of it. I certainly need those men, and could use a dozen more."

"What are you after in particular?"

"Anyone who saw Charley Coombs find that hammer and go to the telephone," Roger said. "He must have found it as the party was approaching the Chassis Shop, so any one of them might have seen it. Charley telephoned from a booth just near the spot where he died."

"Keep at it," urged Knightley. "Any luck with the men who attacked Malcolm M. last night?"

"There are a couple of possibles. I was sending Sheppard to see them when the new thing happened. I won't go to sleep on it."

"It's about half past three," Knightley said, with a chuckle. "I think I'll telephone your wife and say that you'll be late tonight."

"I'll telephone her, because I won't be going home at all," Roger said. "I want to be on the spot. Amory lives only five miles away, Sir Ian and Malcolm much nearer. I may spend the evening checking them one by one."

"I'll send you a few tablets of benzedrine," Knightley said.

Roger rang off. Old Popham was filling out cards, and thoroughly immersed in his job, nothing ever nagged him. Sheppard and the others were out. There was no news of the two suspects for the previous night's attack, nothing specific to do until the hammer was returned, except try to find the explanation of the speed with which Coombs had been killed.

Identifying the owner and the usual place where that hammer was kept was high on the list of urgent jobs, and he was making notes hurriedly when there was a tap at the door.

He called, "Come in," and the door was opened by Tessa Lee.

Chapter Fifteen

The Bright Idea

Roger had an odd thought as the girl came in and closed the door behind her: that he would like to see her smile. He hadn't, yet. She was almost too beautiful when her face was set, as he always saw it. He could see the evidence of strain at her eyes and the tension in her body, and wondered whether she had come without anyone else knowing because of his questions last night, or whether she was simply a messenger. He seemed to see her more clearly. Perhaps that was a trick of the light. Her severe white blouse and black skirt were just right in the circumstances. The blouse was full at the breast, and did nothing to emphasise her figure, even if nothing could conceal it.

"I hope I'm not interrupting," she said.

"Glad to see you," Roger said. "Come and sit down." He felt glad that he was able to relax. The girl was so wholesome to look at, and at least she hadn't pressed that button. But she might have brought an urgent message to the killer; and she might have passed it on to Munro.

Roger had the impression that she would make any sacrifice for the man she loved; then he rejected that as sentimental nonsense. Watch her, watch everyone, and remember that self-interest was the strongest factor in most people.

"Mr Malcolm asked me to come and see you," she said, and answered one question. "He hopes you'll keep what I have to say to yourself."

Half a loaf?

"I will," Roger promised, and took out a packet of cigarettes. "Smoke?"

She looked at a cigarette as if longingly, and then said: "No, thank you, I never smoke during the day. But don't let me stop you."

Roger lit up, as she sat with her back to Popham, who would make shorthand notes of everything she said. "Mr West, is it true that Roy Grannett was murdered while in our hospital?"

"The evidence suggests that he was injured more badly while there," Roger answered.

"So it's no longer true that he died as a result of the incident yesterday lunchtime?"

"It's less certain than it was."

"I hope you'll forgive my questions, but I do want to try to be sure in my mind," Tessa went on hurriedly. "Do you—do you think that ex-Inspector Coombs was murdered, too?"

The world would know by this evening.

"Yes."

"That's what Malcolm said," the girl declared, and closed her eyes, as if she was very tired. Then she opened them with an obvious effort. "I told Mal—Mr Munro what I am going to tell you, Mr West, and he agreed that I should. I have been with the party touring the factory most of the day. As usual, I went ahead to each place they were going to visit, to make sure that the Shop Managers were ready. The management like to make things go very smoothly whenever there is such a tour, especially if Sir Ian is going to be with the party."

Roger nodded. She really had something to say, about what had happened today: and Charley Coombs' murder had happened.

"I went outside again, and they went in. As they passed, Mr Coombs was bending down over a heap of scrap metal. I saw him wrap something in some newspaper, there was a pile waiting nearby to be collected," Tessa said. "He put it under his coat. Did you find anything? "

Was this the real purpose of the visit? Was she, was Malcolm Munro, desperately anxious to find out whether the hammer had been discovered?

"Obviously I can't be sure whether we found anything that Mr Coombs took away until we know what it was like," Roger said. "Can you describe it?"

"I can't be very precise," Tessa said, "but I'm pretty sure it had a handle. He took it from the bottom of the heap, rather gingerly, and wrapped it up quickly, but I believe it was a hammer." She paused, but when Roger didn't interrupt, went on: "I hope that will be useful."

If it were true, it certainly would be; now they had to search for anyone seen to put anything beneath that heap of metal, and for the owner of the hammer.

"All information is useful, Miss Lee. Did you see anyone else near Mr Coombs at the time?"

"No—not really near."

"Near enough to see what he was doing?"

"There were several people," Tessa said, "but I doubt if they noticed anything. I think they were between me and Mr Coombs, and coming away from him. The only person who might have noticed it was Ricky Woods."

"Ricky—" began Roger, and the significance of the name Woods struck home. "The boy who threw the oranges?"

"Yes."

"I didn't know he was back already."

"Mr Munro reinstated him," Tessa said, "and he clocked in about one o'clock. He's a learner-fitter, and acts mostly as a messenger, going from shop to shop. I don't know for sure that he noticed what Mr Coombs took, but he was near enough to."

"Where am I likely to find him now?"

"His headquarters are here, in the Assembly Shop."

"I'll go and see him, right away," Roger said. "Is there anything else, Miss Lee? What message did you take to Mr Munro at the Assembly Shop just before Coombs was killed, for instance?"

"I had a message for Mr Amory."

"What?"

"That the Minister of Labour would like to speak to him about the dispute," Tessa answered, and it was hardly likely that she would lie about that.

"Thank you. Do you, and does Mr Malcolm Munro, think that Mr Torrance is responsible for any of the attacks?" asked Roger, without warning.

Tessa caught her breath.

Roger stood up, and went to her side. She didn't move, but was very pale.

"Well, do you?"

"Of course I don't."

"Did you think it last night?" She didn't answer.

"Did you think Mr Torrance was behind it last night?" Roger demanded sharply.

She said: "No, not really. I couldn't believe it, but—" She was breathing very hard. "But he has many friends in the factory. They hero-worship him. The idea came into my head, and I couldn't get it out."

"What put it in?"

"Nothing in particular."

"Miss Lee, the only thing to help either Mr Torrance or Mr Munro is the truth," Roger said sharply. "Lies, half truths, silences will only make things worse. You recognised one of the men who attacked Mr Munro last night as a friend of Mr Torrance, didn't you?"

She wanted to deny it, but she did not speak at all.

Roger made the final thrust which might make her break down.

"Was it the man I caught and whom Mr Munro helped to escape?"

She nodded; and then told him the man's name. It was Arthur Winn, a night-shift worker already on the suspect list.

When she had gone, Roger made sure that Woods wasn't in the Assembly Shop, then put a general call out, through the Yard, for young Woods, Arthur Winn, and Pegnall, the other night-shift worker.

"Now we want every part of the plant searched," Roger said to Sheppard. "It's got to be a quick, thorough job, and never mind the management."

Tessa Lee went back to her office feeling flat and useless. She hadn't helped Malcolm, and might have made the situation worse. When she thought of the way West had sprung Hugh Torrance's name on her she felt as if she'd tried to hold back the tide.

Did the police suspect Malcolm of Roy Grannett's murder? Did the factory men know for sure? Was that why they had set upon him, taking the law into their own hands?

Or had Hugh Torrance's jealousy and bitter disappointment turned his mind? A murderer had struck twice, and could strike again.

She reached her office at a little after half past four, and was not surprised to see Malcolm's door open at once. He came straight across, slid his arm round her waist, and kissed her.

"I love you, remember? And I don't like that frown. After all, the world knows that you love me, too!"

"Malcolm, we can't talk about this now."

"Oh, yes, we can!" The gleam in his eyes suggested that he was no longer worried either for himself or by what had happened. "I've just been talking to my revered father. A real heart-to-heart. Apart from the fact that he wants me to vote for him on the pay issue, he is showing an unsuspected, very mellow side. Apparently you were heard to declare your love when I was knocked out, sweetheart, and papa was told. We have his qualified approval."

Every other thought was driven out of Tessa's mind.

"You're not just *saying* this, are you?"

"He asks that we wait a year, and I can probably beat him down to six months," said Malcolm, and kissed her forehead. "Three, if I were to vote with him, but I'm still with Amory. We've got to keep everything ticking over here. In spite of the excitement, today's three VIPs ordered a total of three thousand Mark 9s, a cool three million pounds' worth of export money, all in hard currency."

He was so easy in his manner that it was easy to forget the danger. He worked a kind of spell over her.

"Wonderful!"

"That's better. Anyway, we simply can't risk a strike, and I think that we can dissuade the old boy if we go the right way about it. Bob and I are going to have dinner with him tonight."

"Do you seriously think you can persuade him?"

"If we can get it out of his head that what has happened is all part of a conspiracy to put up the backs of the workpeople, yes. That's his obsession. Grannett's the psychological obstacle, of course. Dad is convinced that Grannett wants to call the men out on strike, and even if we give them this increase they'll be after another in a month or so. I'm going to spring a surprise on him," Malcolm added, and his eyes positively glowed.

"How?"

"Grannett will be at home, after dinner. We'll get 'em face to face, and see if they can't sort things out between them."

Tessa said slowly: "Are you sure it will help?"

"It can't make anything worse," Malcolm said dryly. "Both Harrison and Grannett are coming after dinner, there's at least a chance that after this there'll be real harmony."

"Whose idea was it to get Grannett and your father together?"

"Sweetheart, I cannot tell a lie." Malcolm put a hand at his heart dramatically. "It was my very own. Stop worrying, I've a feeling in my bones that Copper West will see us through. What did he have to say?"

It didn't take long to tell.

"He keeps his eyes open and his wits about him," Malcolm said reflectively. "So he was on to Hugh and you."

"Yes. Mal, do you—?"

"No, I do not think Hugh Torrance would touch a thing like this."

"He's always drinking, and he's never himself these days," Tessa found herself saying. "He's done some odd things, darling."

"Not so odd as cracking Roy Grannett's skull in the hospital," Malcolm said. "Yes, that's what happened. I've talked to the Sister and added it all up. There's no reasonable doubt. Hugh might try to kill himself and take me with him, but he wouldn't hire a gang of thugs to do the dirty work."

"I hope to goodness you're right," Tessa said vehemently. "Mal, did you let the man Winn escape last night?"

"Does West know *that?*"

"He guessed. So you did?"

"Yes."

"Then you must be afraid that Hugh is behind it," Tessa said uneasily. "You know that Arthur Winn will do anything Hugh tells him."

"The fact that I was mad last night doesn't stop me from becoming sane today," said Malcolm, "and I'm sane. It wasn't Hugh, that's unthinkable. It's Copper West's job to find out who it was, too, so let's leave it to him. You should have heard Dad trying to be parental over you! Believe it or not, he already has a soft spot for you, he actually said that if he were twenty years younger he would cut me out!"

Malcolm laughed.

Tessa found herself laughing, too.

But deep down, she was still frightened. If it had not been Hugh Torrance, then who was the killer? How much did Malcolm really know?

She was close to the window when she laughed, and Roger, passing at that moment and who had paused to look up at her, saw her. It gave vitality to her beauty, told him that he had been right to wonder what she was like when she smiled.

Now he wondered what made her laugh.

He went to the gatehouse, had a word with a Yard man on duty, and went by a roundabout tour to the Paint Shop. Every available detective was looking for Ricky Woods, who had not been seen leaving by any entrance, or climbing a fence. The gatekeeper had been quite sure that he hadn't gone out this way.

Roger passed the squat Powerhouse, which stood strangely silent, almost as if dead, and entered the Paint Shop by the door through which he had come out this morning. He paused to glance at the little summer-house which marked the original workshop, and remembered the passionate way in which Sir Ian had spoken. Perhaps Grannett didn't realise that this business was almost flesh and blood to old Munro. Perhaps neither of them realised that each was working out of a deep conviction that he was doing the right thing. Someone ought to find a way of bringing them together.

Roger entered the big shop.

It had the same heavy, rather sickly smell of cellulose, every conveyor was working, including the one where there had been the trouble that morning. The same lanky, splay-footed man was on duty near the entrance to the heat tunnel, and the car bodies coming out at the other end were now black and very shiny.

Grannett was at his stand-up desk, with Sheppard next to him.

Grannett looked up without enthusiasm, but also without hostility.

"Come to have another go?" he asked. "I still don't know a thing about it, and I don't know where young Woods is either. He was here just after two o'clock, but I haven't seen him since."

"He hasn't been seen anywhere since," said Sheppard. There was suspicion in the sergeant's voice, and he had pushed his hat to the back of his head, thus showing the whole of the Paint Shop his baldness. He looked hot, too; it was warm in here, as well as noisy.

"What was he doing here?" asked Roger.

"He'd brought some colour orders from the main office," Grannett said. "Wanted to know if I approved of him coming back. I told him he'd been a silly young fool, and that if he ever chucked oranges at a Rolls-Bentley again I'd personally recommend his dismissal. Wasn't too hard on him, he's badly cut up about Roy."

Bitterness crept into Grannett's voice.

"Did you see which way he went from here?"

"I left him at the desk, I was wanted at the other end of the shop. That was the last I saw of him."

"Was Lanky on duty?"

"No, it was his afternoon break. He has it early."

"Who was on duty?"

"One of the charge-hands," said Grannett, "but if you want to know the truth, the charge-hand was probably outside having a draw. You get 'em like that every now and again. Lanky is as reliable as a retriever, but some chaps—" Grannett broke off, and made himself grin. "Now tell me that I'm talking the same language as they do in the board room!"

Roger said: "I'd like to see this charge-hand. Did Woods come here often?"

"Three or four times a day, with colour orders," Grannett said. "Between you and me he was a nuisance. Sneaked out on the tunnel observation platform whenever he could, always wasting time. Something about the heat tunnel fascinated him."

Roger said, slowly: "Could he have gone to that platform today?"

"Almost certainly did."

"Could he have been pushed *into* the heat tunnel?"

Sheppard caught his breath, and Grannett raised his hands and stared as if in horror at the steps which led to the platform. Then he raced to it, yards ahead of Roger or Sheppard.

Lanky stood aside, puzzled, perhaps annoyed.

They crowded on to the tiny platform. Car bodies were passing in their endless stream, sleek and shiny from the new paint. Inside, the fierce temperature was hardening the cellulose so that it would withstand all extremes of weather.

Grannett pressed his face against the observation window, looking right and left and immediately beneath the door, which should be opened only when the tunnel was cool.

Then he said: "Oh, God."

Chapter Sixteen

Face to Face

When the conveyor was stopped and the tunnel cooled off enough to get Ricky Woods' body out it was obvious that the youth had been there for hours. Certainly he had died within a minute or two of entering the tunnel. He had known the control switches, and it was conceivable that he had committed suicide, but much more likely that someone else had pressed the switches, and then pushed him.

Grannett had a dozen witnesses to prove that he hadn't been there when Woods had first gone to the platform. Lanky had been nearby, according to other witnesses, and the unreliable charge-hand had also been near. Both he and Lanky were taken into Elling for questioning.

"Now we want all of Ricky Woods' friends, all the people who saw him today, here and at his home," Roger said. "He saw Coombs get that hammer, we can be reasonably sure that he knew whose it was. He was a weak type, the type who would crack under questioning." Roger spoke in a cold, aloof voice on the telephone to Knightley, about six o'clock that evening. "I'm trying to find out everyone who was near the Paint Shop entrance which I used. It's only a side door, and if Lanky and the charge-hand were gossiping or smoking round the corner, someone could have got in without being seen. It's not likely, but I'm checking."

"Right," Knightley approved. "Got either of the suspects in the attack on Malcolm Munro yet?"

"I'm going to see them myself."

"How's the strike position?"

"So-so. Grannett won't give way, and he seems to know that his real obstacle is Sir Ian," Roger said. "I'm told that the directors are going to have dinner together tonight, and Grannett and Harrison are going to the house afterwards. A get-together like that might yield something. I'm having men back and front of that house."

"Keep it up," Knightley encouraged.

"I'll keep it up," growled Roger. "There's an angle we haven't paid much attention to yet," he went on, "and I don't suppose we can do a lot about it today, now. Who might want to bring the value of Munro stock down, and then cash in?"

"We chaps here think of some things, occasionally," Knightley said. "We've gone into the shareholding position, but I don't know that we've got anything to help. The family or directors own most of the shares, but more and more are being sold. They're quoted lower today than yesterday. There could be a slump, with someone waiting to buy cheap."

"Anyone on the board likely?"

"No. Torrance had a few shares. Biggest single shareholder outside the Board is Harrison – or rather, Harrison and his wife, jointly."

"They well off?"

"I just said they were big Munro shareholders."

Roger grinned.

"Sorry. All right – have they shown any sign of needing money or losing a lot? "

"No," said Knightley, "but we'll keep probing."

"Thanks."

"What's really eating you?" Knightley demanded.

"The fact that everything's happened so fast," Roger said. "First there's a fracas and a bit of a shindy. Within half an hour or so Roy Grannett is dead. Before we can turn round there are two attacks on Munro. Charley makes a discovery, and is dead before we can say snap. Woods turns up at one o'clock, and is dead within an hour. The first affair couldn't have been planned, but the killer was sitting ready to strike, must have been expecting something to break."

Knightley said: "I see what you mean. The killer moves so fast he seems to be in two places at once."

There was a pause. Then: "Say that again," said Roger.

"What?"

"Say that again," Roger urged, and it was as if a flash of light had shown up some of the dark corners of his own mind.

"The killer moves so fast he seems to be in two places at once."

"I've only just seen one obvious thing," Roger said very softly. "We want more than one killer. No single man would have the nerve to keep this up. Roy Grannett, Coombs, Woods, all in twenty-four hours, as well as the attacks on Munro. We want a group of men, with a leader. That's an angle, a group of men, mostly workmen."

"Know who's most likely to be able to get a group together?" Knightley demanded.

"Yes, Torrance."

"Torrance is right," Knightley said. "Handsome, keep cracking on this group inside the plant, if several men are involved, with a different one for each job, it would make sense. Turn Elling inside out for Winn and Pegnall. Check all of Woods' friends, Roy Grannett's, too."

"I will," Roger said roughly.

He rang off, put a call through to Division to step up the hunt for Winn and Pegnall, and then sat motionless at his desk. He felt no easing of the tension, until, for no apparent reason, he thought of his wife. From that moment on he wanted to talk to her, he liked nothing less than being brief with her. But he couldn't see himself getting home tonight. He stubbed out a cigarette abruptly, and put in a call to the Bell Street house. Almost immediately the ringing sound started, he was answered: "Chelsea 01234."

"That's you, Scoop," Roger said, and the pleasant tone of his elder son's voice had already cheered him. "How are you?"

"Oh, I'm fine! I say, Dad!" Now there was excitement in the boy's voice. "I had a wonderful day. You know we had the school sports this afternoon, don't you? ... You'd never believe how many times I came in first ... *Yes, first* ... Five, would you believe it? ... Eh? Oh, the high jump, the 440-yard hurdles, the 440 yards, the 100 yards and throwing the cricket ball, and Richard got a first and two seconds, too. Jolly good, wasn't it?"

"Wonderful!" Roger felt immeasurably more cheerful. "Decide how you'd like to celebrate, and the first Saturday or Sunday I can get off, we'll do it."

"Jolly good," said Scoopy. "As a matter of fact, I've already thought of something, but it's a Wednesday, actually. That International match at Wembley."

"I'll fix it," Roger promised.

"Oh, Dad, thanks a million! Richard! Richard!" Scoopy's voice faded for a moment, obviously as he put his hand over the mouthpiece, and then he went on: "Dad says we can go to the big match, how about that?"

Richard's voice came faintly: "I said he would, didn't I?"

Roger chuckled. Richard, with a slightly higher-pitched voice, came on the line as innocently as a cherub.

"Hallo, Dad, are you coming home before we go to bed tonight? ... Oh, well, I expect you'll see us tomorrow, then—Oo, yes, I was first in the three-legged race, and second in the relay, that is my team was, and in the 440 yards, old Scoop was miles ahead, though ... Yes, thanks, wizard ... Yes, I'll call her."

There was a pause. Then: "Hallo, darling," Janet said. "Did Richard get it right, you'll be home late?"

"Nearly right. I don't think I can make it at all, sweet." He knew that Janet hated him being out at night when involved in a murder case, and the cheerful mood, born out of the children's excitements, could easily be spoiled. Instead, it became even better, for Janet said: "What a shame! But I did wonder if it was wise to come right the way across London if you have to be at the factory again early in the morning. You will get a bed for the night, though, won't you?"

"Oh, yes, that's a promise!"

"And be careful."

"Never more so."

"And I shall let the boys stay up until ten o'clock or so, as a special treat. The rest of the evening won't seem so long, then," Janet said.

Two minutes later Roger rang off, smiling with the contentment of a happy family man. It would take a lot to shake him out of this mood. He turned back to the reports, all of them written out in Popham's careful, precise but rather small handwriting, and was half way through when the telephone bell rang. He glanced up as Popham answered: "Chief Inspector West's office."

He paused.

"Division, sir, Mr Green," he said.

"Thanks." Roger lifted his extension. "Hallo, Green, how are things with you?"

"We've cornered that pair of suspects, Winn and Pegnall, the couple we think had a hand in the attack on young Munro," commenced Green simply.

Roger's mind flared to a question: cornered?

"Got on to them through that night commissionaire you put us on to," Green went on. "He's been at the same pub twice today, and we had a crack at him before he came on duty. He says they paid him a quid to disappear, and swears he didn't know why. Just to clinch it, one of them's the owner of the ballpoint pen we found, the other owned the handkerchief with his monogram on it. Girl friend gave it to him, that's where love can land you. They've gone to earth in a little cafe in Elling North, and bolted the doors on us. It's a lock-up place, only a couple of rooms. We're going to winkle them out now – I thought you'd like to have a chance to be there."

"Thanks. What's the name of the café?"

"Ma's," answered Green. "Any of my chaps will be able to guide you straight over, everyone knows Ma's. Like us to wait until you arrive, or shall we get after 'em?"

"Get 'em if you can," said Roger. "Any risk that they're armed?"

"Oh, they're armed, but only with knives and knuckledusters, as far as I can find out," Green said. "I've got the place surrounded, no fear that they'll escape."

"If you get 'em before I arrive, take 'em straight to the station, and I'll join you there," Roger said. "But don't take any chances, we want them alive. After what's happened here, I'm prepared for anything."

With a local detective officer at his side, Roger reached Ma's Café in twenty minutes. As he turned the corner of the street, he saw a crowd, police cars, uniformed police pushing the crowd back, and an ambulance. He had a momentary fear that the worst had happened, but then he saw two men, each handcuffed, being led from a dreary-looking, lighted café, to a waiting police car. On the pavement was a uniformed policeman, with a nasty cut on his forehead. Roger didn't try to take his car through, but jumped out and hurried to the café, where Green was standing by the injured policeman, and watching the ambulance men put him on to a stretcher.

"How'd it happen?" Roger asked.

"The swine threw knives," Green said. He looked pale and tired in the poor light. "They were a pretty dangerous pair to have round the Munro plant. Took six of us to overpower them, they didn't mean to be taken if they could avoid it."

"Well, you got 'em," Roger said softly. "Now all we've got to do is make them talk."

Chapter Seventeen

Home Ground

Roger did not get a close-up of the two men until they were at the Elling Police Station, being charged. Arthur Winn had big shoulders and a bull neck, and was a picture of a Dickens brute, even to broken teeth and a cauliflower ear. His right eye was swollen, and there was a small cut at his lips, on the left-hand side. He wore old jeans and a khaki sweater with a roll collar. One of the Division's biggest men was handcuffed to him, and a second plain-clothes man stood on his other side. Any moment, he might start fighting again. He didn't answer a single question, not even to confirm his name.

The other prisoner was slighter, and looked much less tough. He was clean-shaven, and wore a suit and a collar and tie. In the fight he had split his right ear, and badly hurt his left hand, which was bound up with a handkerchief.

He admitted to the name of Robert Pegnall.

"Now let's have it, Pegnall," Green said, "who put you up to attacking Munro? You'd no personal reason."

"My hands hurt awful," Pegnall said, in a whining voice, "I want to see a doctor."

"You'll see a doctor, and you'll be lucky if you don't see an undertaker before this is over," Green rasped. "Let's have the truth. Who paid you to attack Munro?"

"If I don't see a doctor, I'll complain to the court," whined Pegnall. "You've no right to keep a wounded man standing here while you ask him questions, it's not lawful."

"Here's a man who knows all about the law," Roger put in mildly. "It's not lawful to join with others in an attack on another man. It's not lawful to smash a man's skull in with a hammer." He waited to let that sink in, and saw Winn's eyes open wide, and Pegnall's lips tighten. "It's not lawful to release a chassis and crush a man to death, and it's not lawful to push a man into the heat tunnel so that he fries. But it's all been done."

Winn said in a strained voice: "We never did it!"

"You keep your trap shut," Pegnall said, the whine quite gone. "They can talk their heads off, they haven't got anything on us."

"Please yourself," said Roger. "You've got ten years apiece coming to you for the two jobs we know you did, and you'll be lucky if you don't hang for the others. But if you talk you might make it easier for yourselves."

"I tell you we never touched no one else!" Winn's voice, now high-pitched, made him sound almost like an imbecile.

"Perhaps you didn't, but it wasn't made to look that way," Roger said roughly. "Three murders make quite a count, and as things stand we'll get you on one of them. But if you'd rather wait in the cooler, please yourselves. Talk a bit now, and we'll find you a comfortable chair and a cigarette or two." He turned to Green. "Take 'em down to the cells, and have a look at the small one's hand. If he needs a doctor you'd better arrange it."

"I'd rather fetch a vet," Green said, moving towards the door.

"Listen, West," Winn said, in the same high-pitched voice. "We didn't croak anyone, we only—"

"Shut your trap!" Pegnall rasped.

"We only beat up Munro, that's all we did, no one never told me it was a murder rap. We never killed no one— anyway *I* didn't."

"Who paid you?" Roger asked sharply.

Pegnall exclaimed: "I paid him, that's all you want to know."

"You crazy?" Winn asked, and looked at him as if he thought he was mad. "If this is a murder rap I'm talking. It was Mike Grannett who paid us, Mr West. He give us a hundred nicker apiece in advance, and promised another hundred if we made a real mess of Munro!"

"That's wonderful," breathed Green. "That's all we wanted to know."

He looked on top of the world.

"If it's the truth we'll soon find out," Roger said, and felt oddly heavy-hearted, because it wasn't the answer he wanted. "Find 'em chairs and cigarettes, and feed them if they need it, will you?"

"It's against my principles, but I will," Green said, and passed on the orders to a sergeant. Then he followed Roger to the door. "That's got Grannett as tight as we'll ever get him. Going to pick him up right away?"

"I'm going to have a talk to him," said Roger. "You coming, or shall I take Sheppard?"

"I've got too much Divisional stuff to do, but thanks for offering."

"Pity. I'll have Sheppard later," Roger said. "I'd better go back to the factory and see how things are there."

He didn't go to the factory, but drove towards Elling Hill, the residential part of the suburb, where Sir Ian lived in the big old house. It took twenty minutes to find the house called Munro, for Roger was confused by streets and wide drive entrances. Harrison's big, elderly Daimler was outside, and in front of it stood a motorcycle.

That would be Grannett's.

Roger wondered what was happening now that Sir Ian and Grannett were face to face.

One thing was certain: Grannett could have organised it all, no one was in a better position for that.

Even before Grannett and Harrison had arrived, Malcolm Munro had felt uneasily that the experiment was going to be a flop. His father was more adamant than ever; throughout dinner and immediately afterwards he resolutely refused to concede the need for reconciliation or compromise.

"Got to fight them," he said flatly. "It's got to come sooner or later. Got to let them know who's master."

It was useless to keep saying that he was living in the past.

"I still feel that they'd take an offer, and that if they did ask for more in a few months you'd have a much better case for refusing," Amory argued.

"The case is good enough now," insisted Sir Ian. "No, Bob, my mind is absolutely made up. I won't be blackmailed, and I won't be pushed around."

Malcolm was finding it difficult even to hide his exasperation.

"Give me some more coffee, and put plenty of milk in it, that was as bitter as aloes," said Sir Ian. Malcolm poured out, and handed him the cup. His father drank again, quickly as always, and there came a footstep outside the door. "I warn you I shall give Grannett the raw edge of my tongue if he's impertinent."

"Remember he's coming at my invitation," Malcolm said.

"No reason why he shouldn't behave himself," his father retorted.

A manservant opened the door.

"Colonel Harrison and—ah—Mr Grannett, sir," he announced. The pause before and the slur of 'Mr' was obviously deliberate on the part of a tall, pale-faced footman, but Grannett appeared not to notice. He came in without haste, a little behind Harrison, wearing a neatly pressed navy-blue suit, a soft white collar. The firelight glinted on his rimless glasses and red hair.

"Ah, George, come in. Grannett." Sir Ian looked at the shop steward as if at a laboratory specimen.

Malcolm pushed up a chair.

"What will you have to drink?" he asked. Brandy glasses were warming, liqueur glasses stood on a silver tray by the side of a dozen bottles ranging from Drambuie to Cointreau.

"Just a cup of coffee, please," Grannett said.

"Brandy, George?" Sir Ian looked at Harrison.

"Thanks. Yes." Harrison sounded abrupt, and looked like a bleached effigy of a soldier, and the dark bags under his eyes made him appear to glare.

Sir Ian picked up his coffee, sipped, grunted, put the coffee down, and took a saccharin tablet from a jewelled snuffbox. Grannett put his coffee down close to the old man's.

After a pause, Amory started the ball rolling, pleasantly enough. The only purpose of this informal talk was to try to avoid the strike. Sir Ian listened, pulling his collar as if it were much too tight, and drinking his coffee.

"Damn thing's choking me," he said abruptly, and tugged. "Well, let's hear what you have to say, Grannett."

Grannett put his case concisely and without emphasis, but Sir Ian did not even let him finish properly.

"Nothing you've said is new, or justifies the claim for an increase," he declared arrogantly. "We don't know how Mark 9 will turn out yet. Early signs are favourable, but there could be a recession in world markets or another crisis at home. Any one of a dozen things could turn the tide the other way. The wage bill is already higher than the company can safely stand."

"Absolutely right," Harrison approved.

"I know that things are not as favourable as Grannett seems to think, but we have a year's orders for Mark 9 on the list," Amory said.

"And will lose half of 'em if we don't deliver to time. And if we have more of the kind of delays we've been having these past few days, we're bound to be late."

"I know, but that isn't Grannett's fault. He—"

"Perhaps he'll be good enough to prove it," said Sir Ian.

Malcolm raised his hands, as if in surrender. Harrison, paler than ever, took his cigar from his mouth, looked at the half-inch of pale-grey ash, and then put it back again.

Grannett, sitting in a small armchair and showing no sign of embarrassment, paused for a moment, then stood up and smoothed down his coat. He was wearing a black tie and a wide black armband.

"It's obvious I'm only wasting my time here," he said, in his deliberate, restrained voice. "I can only hope you other gentlemen can persuade Sir Ian that the men will strike if the claim isn't met."

"I take it they will consider an offer," Amory put in quickly.

"They might, but it would have to be a good one." Grannett nodded to Sir Ian and the others. "Good night." He turned towards the door, and Malcolm went to it with him, opened it, and preceded him on to the landing.

Sir Ian did just say: "Good night," but Harrison kept silent.

Malcolm closed the door. A big chandelier, burning forty electric-lamp bulbs, spread a soft glow about the white panelling, and the pictures which were worth a fortune. Grannett looked round with a kind of smile which wasn't easy to understand, and said: "Oil and water don't mix, that's about the truth of it, Mr Munro."

"It was my idea that you should come here," said Malcolm ruefully. "Just another of my mistakes. I'm sorry it turned out such a complete flop."

"The trouble with your father is that he's still living fifty, years ago," Grannett said. "It's true of a lot of big employers, too. They don't realise it, but we're no longer in the days of unemployment and starvation wages and patronising owners, but in an age when a man insists on getting a fair wage for a fair day's work. If you look at the output per man in the factory, Mr Munro, you'll find that it's higher than anywhere else in the motor car industry, and that's a fact. You've got a lot of damned good workers, and they give the fair day's work. They mean to have the rest of it fair, too."

They were nearly at the foot of the stairs.

"I still hope we can put off a strike," Malcolm said. "If we get one, I shall still feel that it was my fault."

Grannett turned to look at him, straightly.

"Because of my brother? I shouldn't worry about that any longer, Mr Munro. Oh, I was bitter about it at first, I don't mind admitting, but I've seen more of you today, and I've also weighed things up a bit better. You lost your head once yesterday, and I lost mine later. Now we've both learned from the experience. There are just two men who stand in the way of the wage increase and good labour relations *and* record output. That's your father and Colonel Harrison. If you and the others can't make them see reason, don't blame anyone else, Mr Munro."

They were standing in the hall when the front-door bell rang, almost as a climax to Grannett's words. A door opened, not far off, but Malcolm didn't wait for a servant to come: he opened the door himself.

Roger West stood on the doorstep.

"Don't tell me you've even followed me here," Grannett said, as if exasperated. "You can't work night *and* day."

"Only until the job's finished," Roger said. "There have been more than enough tragedies in this affair to risk another." He paused, but obviously had more to say, and the others waited. "Grannett, a man named Arthur Winn, a night-shift labourer in the Paint Shop, says you paid him and another man to round up the gang which attacked Mr Munro last night. Three, including Winn, attacked Mr Munro again later. What have you to say?"

Grannett looked utterly dumbfounded.

But it was neither he nor Malcolm Munro who spoke next: it was Harrison, who came rushing to the landing, calling out in a desperate voice.

"Malcolm, fetch Dr Jeffrey! Your father's been taken ill, don't lose a moment."

Chapter Eighteen

Runaway

Harrison stood at the top of the stairs, looking like a ghost.

Grannett, still shocked, was in the front doorway. Roger was between him and the Divisional plain-clothes man watching the front of the house; there was another at the back. Malcolm turned to stare at Harrison as if he couldn't believe what he said, but sight of the Works Manager must have convinced him. He swung round.

"Doctor's across the road," he said, and pushed past Roger and ran. A street-light showed his disappearing figure, and a Yard man after him. Harrison moved away from the head of the stairs, while Grannett stood staring at Roger, his grey-green eyes still rounded as if in disbelief. It would be easy to believe that he had not realised what the shouting was about; that he could think only of Roger's abrupt question.

A woman's voice sounded from the stairs: Tessa Lee's.

"Let me see if I can help."

Vaguely came Harrison's voice: "He looks—dreadful." Grannett gripped Roger's arm, with fingers so powerful that the pressure hurt.

"If Winn told you that, he lied."

"Do you know a Robert Pegnall?"

"Yes."

"He's at the police station with Winn. They've been accused of the attack on Munro yesterday, and both say you paid them to do it."

Grannett said again: "It's a lie, West," but his voice trailed off.

Upstairs, a man said: "It can't be," in a hopeless kind of way, and his voice carried only because all the doors were open.

Torn between racing up to find out what had happened, and trying to judge the effect of the accusation on Grannett, Roger turned towards the plain-clothes man.

"Wait here with Mr Grannett, will you? Grannett, I want to talk to you again before you go." Roger turned and ran for the stairs, hearing the mutter of voices in a room which seemed to be on the left of the landing. He reached the open door. There was a kind of tableau, set in a frame of much beauty; fine bookcases, lovely pictures, wine-red velvet curtains, a richly coloured carpet, a coal fire with the firelight flickering on brandy glasses, on the polished furniture, and on Sir Ian, who was on the floor.

Gathered about him were two men and the girl, all standing back, appalled. The old man's back was arched, and he seemed to be touching the floor only with his head and his heels. His pupils were dilated so that his eyes looked staring and blank. There was only one explanation of that awful spasm, and Roger knew exactly what it was.

Sir Ian had been poisoned with strychnine.

The girl noticed Roger, and asked despairingly: "Is there anything I can *do?*"

"Get boiling water ready, bowls and towels, prepare a bedroom quickly, and get a servant to find out if there's any permanganate of potash in the house." Roger spun round, and saw a landing window close to him, and lights some little way off, probably across the street. He opened the window, and the chilly night air struck cold against his forehead. Now he could see Malcolm standing against the light which streamed from a house nearly opposite; he could see the Yard man, too.

He shouted: "Munro! Can you hear me?"

There was a pause, but Munro swung round on the porch.

"*Monro!*"

"I can hear you!"

"Tell the doctor to bring a strychnine antidote."

"What?"

"A strychnine antidote!"

"Got it!" Munro shouted, and turned and seemed to dive into the house across the road. The Yard man who had plunged after him was standing close by; a man to mark for future promotion, he was as close as Munro's shadow. Roger wiped his forehead and turned round. He was ten yards from the door of the room where Sir Ian lay, and the light shone out, but he heard nothing. He reached the doorway, and saw the room empty except for Sir Ian, who seemed to be coming out of the convulsion. Where were the others? Roger glanced round and saw Harrison approaching. Then Sir Ian collapsed and lay flat on his back. He looked dreadful, although his pupils were contracted now.

Roger went across and knelt by his side.

"It's all right," he said very quiedy. "The doctor's on his way, sir. You'll be all right."

The old man, the dynamic old man, the founder and creator of Munro's, the reactionary, the industrial visionary, the vigorous, forceful, dominating, and domineering old throwback, was weak and helpless. His eyes were half closed, as if he were going to lose consciousness; the pain had been dreadful beyond words, Roger knew, and during the spasm Munro had been fully conscious, of everything.

"Do you know what you took?" Roger said. "Do you know if anyone gave you—"

"Coff—ee," Sir Ian said, in a sighing voice. "Very strong—coff—ee. Always take—saccharin. Did—didn't sweeten properly, took—another. The—the doctor will be here soon, won't he?" he pleaded.

"Any moment now," Roger said, and hated himself for going on: "Did anyone put anything into your coffee?"

"Anyone?" asked Sir Ian, vaguely. His eyes closed. "Anyone? That Grannett man, he's a devil. Mustn't give way. Must hold out. Once we give way—"

A cold breeze came into the room, as if the front door had opened and closed quickly; and almost on the instant the old man's body quivered. His hands moved, he gripped Roger's, he cried: "No more, can't stand more, can't—"

And then the sound was strangled in his throat and he went into another convulsion, while men ran up the stairs.

Tessa Lee stood in the doorway, carrying water and towels, appalled.

The old man's pupils were enormously dilated, he seemed to stare at Roger, as if pleading for a relief from pain.

A small, grey man came hurrying, with a pad in his hand and a small blue bottle in the other. "Mind away."

"Sorry." Roger moved. The sickly smell of chloroform came, suddenly overpowering, and made him gasp. He stood up. The doctor was pressing the pad over the old man's mouth and nose, knowing exactly what he should do and doing it expertly. Gradually the convulsions eased, and the old man's eyes closed gently.

The doctor said: "We'll do gastric lavage. Get me a big jug of warm water, boiled if possible." He opened a small leather case which he'd dumped on the floor, and took out another small bottle. "Was it you who shouted for the antidote?"

"Yes."

"Then you know what you're about. Mix half a teaspoonful of this in a gallon of water, no more; make it a third of a teaspoonful. I'll get the stomach pump." He looked up at Tessa. "Need a big bowl or a bucket," he said, and then saw Malcolm, who seemed utterly lost and alone in the doorway, his face set, his eyes staring at the limp figure of the father who was so close to death. "Help her," the doctor ordered, as if he knew that the younger man needed something to do.

The young couple went hurrying out.

"Shouldn't think there's a chance in a thousand," the doctor said to Roger. "If I'd had any sodium amytal I'd have brought it and tried an intravenous, but there's none at the house, only at the surgery. Mind telling me who you are?"

"I'm from Scotland Yard."

"Well, you've got a case on your hands," said the doctor. "I'll stake my last pound that Sir Ian wouldn't commit suicide, and it certainly wasn't an accident, so you're looking for a murderer."

He talked as if Sir Ian was already dead.

"Yes," Roger said, and stirred the potassium permanganate briskly, having it ready as the girl and Malcolm Munro returned. "Must leave you to it," he said then, and straightened up. As he reached the door, Malcolm stretched out a hand, appealingly.

"Will he—?" he began.

"I don't think there's much hope," Roger said. "He was poisoned, almost certainly within the last hour. He said his coffee was very bitter tonight I'll need to question everybody here."

"You'll have a job," Malcolm Munro said. "Harrison and Bob Amory have gone chasing after Grannett, with one of your chaps. Grannett took to his heels."

Roger went towards the landing and the stairs as fast as he had ever moved in his life.

A few minutes before, Grannett had been standing in the hall with one Divisional detective, looking out into the garden, his stocky, powerful figure hunched, the porch light glinting on his narrowed eyes. He could hear sounds above him, and could hear West's voice, as plainly as if West was still speaking. On the drive was another detective, a biggish man.

Grannett had hardly moved, even when he heard a cry from outside.

That took him completely by surprise. The two detectives jerked their heads round as the cry was repeated, low-pitched but coming clearly to their ears. One of the detectives shone a torch, and a powerful beam of light shone out and then lost itself in the darkness, but it fell upon a man who began to move to one side.

There were running footsteps from the house across the road. First, the doctor, then Malcolm Munro.

Face set and hard, Grannett moved to let them pass as soon as they arrived. He saw the man outside draw nearer, and then caught a glimpse of him. It was Colonel Harrison, his ever-bright eyes shimmering.

There was a gun in Harrison's hand.

A detective ordered: "Put that gun down at once."

Amory called out from behind Harrison: "Don't be a fool, George! The police will handle Grannett."

For a split second, Harrison and Grannett stared at each other, and there was murder in the Works Manager's eyes. Then Munro raced in on the heels of the doctor, and Harrison was cut off from Grannett's view. Grannett swung round and ran towards a door at the side of the stairs, leading to the servants' quarters. He heard a shout, and guessed that the detectives had started after him. He pulled the door open and entered a narrow, brightly lit passage. The door slammed behind him. He reached another doorway and a middle-aged woman stood gaping at him.

"Where's the back door?" Grannett asked swiftly. "Quick, where is it?"

"Through—through there." The woman pointed to a passage which turned right, off this. He sprang towards it. There was the back door, and a strong breeze was blowing along the passage. There were footsteps, then a detective's voice, demanding: "Where did that man go?"

Grannett reached the door. It was locked but not bolted or chained, and he turned the heavy key and pulled it wide open, on to darkness. He ran out on to a paved courtyard, and then light shone dimly from a window which he couldn't see, and more shone farther afield, from a street-lamp. He could just make out shrubs, trees and bushes, and what looked like a high wall. If he made for the street he would have to run towards the front of the house, and Harrison. He heard footsteps; and then Amory calling again sharply: "George!"

A detective appeared in the doorway through which Grannett had come. Grannett ran headlong for the bushes and trees, and they gave him some cover. Now that he was more used to the light, he could make out the five-foot wall. He tried to see whether there was broken glass or spikes at the top, but could not, and he made a running jump for it, hands outstretched to clutch the top. They fell upon rough concrete. He held on, and then scrambled over, hearing other men in the shrubbery now, heavy breathing, someone muttering. For a moment he was astride the wall, a clear silhouette against it; and that was the moment when a bright flash appeared in the shrubbery. He saw only the sudden, yellow light, and knew that he had been fired at. He heard the bullet strike the wall as he dropped down. There was another sharp crack and flash as he landed on grass; here, the garden was clearer, and he could see the gate of the next house leading to the street. He ran across it in a straight line, ignoring the risk of being shot at from the wall.

Harrison fired again, as if wildly. Grannett heard only the bark of the shot. He reached the gate and vaulted it, and as he swayed on the pavement, looked round towards the cars and his motor-cycle. A detective was running towards him, he had no more than fifty yards' start.

He turned and ran, towards the wide streets and the narrow streets beyond, towards the fields behind Elling, and towards the factory where the night shift was working, and where the floodlit loading and unloading platforms were crowded with men, and from which a glow spread far and wide in the sky.

Chapter Nineteen

The Chase

Roger reached the porch as a shot came from his left. He ran towards the sound, and caught sight of two men, probably Harrison and Amory, disappearing round a corner.

Roger saw a flash and heard another shot, then saw Harrison against the light of the flash. Only a few yards from him was Amory.

Roger called out clearly: "Stop that shooting!"

There came another shot, and Roger saw Harrison trying to haul himself to the top of the wall, with Amory pulling him down.

Outside in the street, a police whistle sounded shrill and loud.

Amory got hold of Harrison's right arm, but couldn't wrench the gun away. Roger reached up, and twisted; the gun dropped. Harrison kicked and struck out, swearing viciously, but they forced him against the wall. Suddenly he collapsed, as if all his strength had gone. Roger let him go, bent down, and groped for the gun. He straightened up, putting it in his pocket, and said to Amory: "Can you manage him?"

"Yes, he'll be all right now."

"Get him back to the house, will you?" Roger asked. "I'll join you."

The police whistle sounded again, loud and alarming in the clear night. Running footsteps faded into the distance. Roger climbed the wall and ran across the lawn. When he reached the street, he saw a uniformed policeman disappearing round a corner; no one else was in sight, and until the whistle shrilled out again there was no other sound.

He ran to his car.

A Yard man was standing nearby, the man from the back of the house.

"Colonel Harrison and Mr Amory came out the back way, and I followed them to the front," he said, anxious to clear himself. "Harrison had a gun and was after Grannett, who ran for it. One of our chaps went after him, so I thought one of us had better stay here, sir."

"Quite right," Roger said. "Go upstairs, get all the coffee cups and glasses and bottles from the library, and lock 'em up so that no one can touch them. Clear?"

"Yes, sir!"

"Then phone the Division for help, and don't let anyone else leave."

"Right!"

Roger got into the car, started the engine, and sent the car shooting forward, its engine roaring. He remembered Torrance and the near-fatality of the morning. He reached the corner and swung the wheel to the left, the way the policeman had turned. The bright beam of his headlamps showed the man at another corner; and as he drove along, Roger saw that there were turnings to both right and left, all drive entrances, and a dozen directions in which the runaway could have gone. Then he saw a solitary figure in plain clothes come dejectedly out of one of the gateways.

Roger stopped.

"Hallo, sir."

"Lost him?"

"Sorry, sir."

"Can't be helped, and he won't get far," said Roger. "We'll go and pick up that copper, and get him back to his beat. Hop in." The plain-clothes man climbed in by his side, and Roger went on: "Call the Yard on the radio for me, will you?" The man flicked the radio on, and soon the voice of a Yard Information Room sergeant came loudly into the car. "West here. Give me Mr Kimbell," Roger said.

There was a moment's pause before Kimbell came on the line, mumbling as if he was chewing. "That you, Handsome? Got it all solved?"

"I've got a runaway to pick up in a hurry," Roger said. "Will you call the Divisional chaps right away and ask for a net to be spread round the Elling Hill area as quick as they can make it? We're looking for Michael Grannett."

"He was my man from the start." Kimbell sounded smug.

"And in case he grabs a car or a bike, you'd better ask them to warn the men at the factory to look out for him, and also put out a general call," Roger said. "Ask 'em to send a couple of men to his home, will you?"

"Right. Is he armed?"

"Not as far as I know."

"Desperate?"

"Could be," said Roger. "Here's another piece of cheer. Sir Ian Munro is dying of strychnine poisoning at his home, and Colonel Harrison seems to have decided that Grannett was the poisoner, and started shooting at him. Care to send a team over pronto?"

"Strewth, you've got quite a circus. Okay, I'll fix it. Say, Handsome."

"Yes?"

"Needn't come in for a meal tonight, baked jam roll's off."

"I'll be lucky if I get a sandwich," Roger said. "Did Knightley tell you about the possibility of a share racket?"

"Possibly is as far as we can go."

"Listen," urged Roger. "Harrison could be charged with shooting with intent to kill. That's excuse enough to get a search warrant for his place. Torrance is in hospital, you ought to be able to fix a look at his flat. Try 'em both, will you, for any evidence of buying Munro Motors stock, or dealings with brokers."

"I'll see what we can do. How about Amory?"

"Amory and Malcolm rate, too, but I doubt if you'll get into their places yet. The first two will do for a start."

"Okay," Kimbell said.

Roger rang off, and pushed his hand through his hair, impatiently, as the constable hurried to the car.

"Hop in, and I'll take you back," Roger said.

"Thank you, sir. Sorry I lost him. There are five different roads just here, though, once he got this far I knew we wouldn't have much of a chance."

"You did all you could." Roger sounded much more philosophical than he felt. "I've sent to your HQ. You stand by until you get special instructions."

"Yes, sir."

"Now, just what happened back at the house?" Roger asked the plain-clothes officer.

The man told his story again in greater detail. Obviously Harrison, with the gun, had really jolted Grannett into running. Had he run out of fear for his life? Did he know about Harrison's medical history? Had he realised that Harrison might be mad?

Mad?

They drew up outside Sir Ian Munro's house.

"I hope not to be more than ten minutes," Roger said. "Stay here."

The plain-clothes man jumped out and opened the door and said: "Yes, sir."

The other, who had stayed at the house, was standing by the front door, which was now closed. "Doctor still here?" Roger asked.

"Yes, sir."

"Lock up those things?"

"In a linen cupboard, sir, I've the key."

"Keep it, and give it to the Yard team that's on its way. Everyone else still here?"

"Yes, sir."

"Thanks," Roger said. He rang the bell, and had to wait nearly three minutes before a manservant answered the door and said almost before he could see who it was: "I'm sorry, Sir Ian can see no one tonight."

Was he covering up because he thought it the best thing to do, or because he'd had instructions?

"Chief Inspector West," Roger said, and the man stepped aside hastily. "Thanks. Where is everybody?"

"The—the doctor and Miss Lee are upstairs in the library, sir, the others are downstairs in the morning-room."

"Mr Munro, Mr Amory, and Colonel Harrison?"

"Not Colonel Harrison, sir. He left ten minutes ago, sir."

"My man said—" Roger began.

"He left by the side door, sir."

He should have had at least four men here earlier, Roger knew. If anything else went wrong he could only blame himself. Even when he had left Harrison to Amory, he had taken the wrong choice; he should not have gone after Grannett.

Roger went back to his car in a hurry, flicked on the radio, and said to the Yard Information Room: "Put an emergency call out for Colonel Harrison of Munro Motors. He's on the rampage in Elling, probably in killing mood."

"We'll see that Mr Kimbell's told, sir."

"Thanks." Roger went back to the house, and the footman watched him go upstairs. When he reached the library door Tessa Lee was just coming out. He remembered thinking how much he would like to see her smile, and that he had seen her laughing. Now, she looked tired, almost a tragic figure, and her eyes closed at sight of him, as if he was the last straw. The doctor was coming out of the room behind her.

"Has he gone?" Roger asked, almost wearily.

"Yes," the doctor said. He looked old and tired, too, as if he had just finished a testing fight. "I'm informing the local police."

"Thank you," Roger said. "But there'll be a party here from Scotland Yard very soon." He looked at the door, saw the key in the lock, and took it out. Sir Ian's body still lay on the floor, covered by a rug; the doctor had known that nothing should be touched. Roger went to the window and saw a man on duty at the back standing only a few yards away. He opened the window, told the man to stay there, then went out of the room and locked the door. The doctor and the girl were at the foot of the stairs, and the doctor was saying: "You really ought to go home and get some sleep, or you'll knock yourself up."

"Oh, I'm all right," Tessa said, and there seemed more spirit in her manner. "I can't go until I know whether Mr Munro wants anything else."

"All right. Tell them I'll be in again later, will you?" The doctor nodded to Roger. "Good night, and thanks." He went out, and Roger and the girl stood together, close to the door of a room where men were talking in undertones: the sound of their voices was just audible.

"Were you in the room when they had coffee?" Roger asked.

"No."

"Where were you?"

"I was typing some letters in the morning-room. Where the others are now. The directors were going to have a letter handed to every foreman and charge-hand in the morning, to try to stop the strike. It was Mr Amory's suggestion."

She spoke jerkily, and Roger knew she was fully aware of two possibilities. Malcolm Munro might be next; or might be the murderer.

If she really accepted the second one, she couldn't believe that Grannett was guilty.

"Has anyone talked about what happened?" Roger asked.

"No."

"Has anyone said who gave Sir Ian the poison?" Her answer came slowly. "Colonel Harrison said that Sir Ian named Grannett."

"Thank you. Miss Lee, do you know of anyone on the Board who has been trying to acquire shares from the company's shareholders?"

She looked surprised.

"No, not really."

"What does that mean?"

"There is often a little buying from distant relations, and adjustments whenever a shareholder dies."

"Has any particular individual always been very anxious to buy lately, while the price has been down?"

"No."

She was quite emphatic, so Roger dropped the subject, and asked: "Are you coming into this session?"

"Not unless you want me to."

"Do something for me instead, will you?" Roger asked. "Get them to make me a couple of sandwiches, I'll eat them in the kitchen as soon as I'm through."

"Yes, of course," Tessa Lee said. And smiled.

She didn't feel like smiling as she went to a small room near the kitchen, dropped into a chair, and stared blankly in front of her.

Sir Ian dead, of poison.

Malcolm present when he had died.

It had been Grannett, it must have been.

But …

Supposing it hadn't been?

What lay behind this awful spate of killing? Why was Malcolm always in a position to have committed the crime? In the hospital, in the Chassis Shop, in the Paint Shop, and here in this very house.

Why had he let Winn escape last night?

Could Hugh Torrance really hate him so much as to try to have him blamed?

Roger opened the door of the morning-room without knocking, but all he heard was what sounded like: "I don't know where he's gone." Obviously that applied to Colonel Harrison. Amory stood with his back to an electric fire, tall and commanding; Malcolm sat on the arm of a chair, drawing at a cigarette. They were trying to put up a show of .stoic calm, but they couldn't be feeling very good.

Amory was the first to speak. "Did you get Grannett?"

"No, but we will, before long."

"I've heard that kind of talk before," growled Malcolm. "I thought you people always got results."

"We get results, and we'll get them this time. Who let Harrison go?"

"I'm afraid I'm to blame," said Amory. "I thought he had calmed down – he often has these excitable outbursts, but they seldom last for long."

"If he gets Grannett, good luck to him," said Malcolm. "If you'd found out that Grannett was behind all this before, my father would still be alive." He sounded bitter and hostile.

"Malcolm, no one could have worked harder than Mr West in the short time at his disposal," Amory interpolated. "Mr West, I'm afraid we're all badly shaken and upset."

"I think I know how everyone feels," Roger said. "I also know that if Colonel Harrison or anyone else tries to take the law into his own hands, he'll run into a lot more trouble than he expects. What made him go berserk?"

"Haven't you anything to think with?" Malcolm demanded.

Amory spread his hands and said: "He felt sure that Grannett put the poison in Sir Ian's coffee."

"Are you also sure?"

"Who else could have done?" Malcolm asked tartly.

"There were five people present," Roger said. "The last one I would expect to commit a murder in those circumstances would be Grannett – he would be sticking his neck out too far. Any reason to believe that he's a fool?"

Malcolm looked taken aback.

"I know that he's a desperate man," Amory said. "Only Sir Ian stood between him and the success he's always dreamed of. If he wins this wage claim for the workpeople, he'll become one of the big figures in the Trade Union Movement. Much more than you might think depends on his success."

Malcolm couldn't wait to exclaim: "Are you seriously accusing one of *us*, West?"

"I'm not yet taking Grannett's or anyone's guilt for granted," Roger said.

"After this, you must be crazy!"

"Think he killed his own brother?" Roger flashed.

"I think he's ruthless enough to kill anyone who gets in his way."

"How did his brother get in his way?"

Malcolm said: "We don't know everything yet."

"I think I know why Roy Grannett was killed," put in Amory very quietly. "I think it was in order to stir up the factory workers to a point of anger and resentment, and so make sure that they would stand out for the wage increases, even if it came to a strike. I think he was killed as a sacrifice, whether it was done with his brother's knowledge or not I neither know nor guess. I do know that his brother saw him when he was lying, drowsy and half conscious, in the hospital. I think that the quarrel which had been forced upon Mr Munro here created the chance to victimise and to vilify him. And I think Sir Ian was as sure of this, and that it was the real cause of his adamance. He was always a man of firm convictions. I believe that Grannett realised that if Sir Ian held out there would be a strike and the comparative failure of his own efforts."

Roger said: "Torrance was half drunk, and crazy enough to risk his own life in what looked like an attempt on Mr Munro's. How do you account for that?"

"That was a personal score."

"Why do you think Coombs was killed?"

"I have little doubt that he found out who killed Roy Grannett."

"And Woods?"

"I think that Woods committed suicide," answered Amory. "In fact, I believe that it was he who actually killed Roy Grannett, Mr West. I think you will find that he comes from a fanatically Communist family, even if he did appear to be so mild-mannered, and that he was more responsible than we realised for the original cause of the trouble. He realised that it was only a matter of time before he was found out."

Malcolm said sharply on the last word: "Have you any better ideas, West?" He was aggressive, almost rude, and that might be because he was still suffering from shock. "Woods had the chance to kill Roy Grannett—"

"Woods didn't have a chance to kill Coombs," Roger retorted. "An investigation team will be here from the Yard at any time," he added. "They'll want to know everything that happened here this evening. I want a broader picture. One director is dead, another has been murderously attacked, and three men at the plant have been killed."

"Are you *telling* us this?" Malcolm asked abruptly.

"I'm reminding you, and pointing out that both management and men have been killed. There is probably a single motive." Roger gave the others a chance to speak, but this time they let it pass. "I've reason to believe that different men have been involved in the murders," Roger went on, "a group of them."

"But why?" demanded Amory.

"There *must* be different motives," Malcolm said.

"It's hardly likely. Mr Munro, we know that Mr Torrance believes he has a reason for personal vengeance. Has anyone else?" When they didn't answer, he went on: "Or has anyone tried to acquire a larger interest in the company?"

It was Amory who said: "Yes, Colonel Harrison. But—"

He was explaining that Harrison acquired every share he could over the years when the team arrived from Scotland Yard.

It took Roger ten minutes to brief the teams, five more to bolt down sandwiches and coffee, three to reach his car and make sure that the search for Harrison and Grannett was stepped up. Then the Yard Information Room said: "Mr Kimbell would like a word with you, sir."

"Put me through."

"Yes, sir—"

"Hallo, Handsome!" When Kimbell came on he was unusually excited. "You're a lucky swab, it's falling into your lap. Harrison's been buying up every share he could from distant relations for years. His wife lost her nerve when our chaps went to her home. She knew that hubby was working to bring Munro stock down and buy all he could at bottom, and apparently Sir Ian had suspected it. And in Harrison's bedroom we found strychnine in tablets which look like saccharin."

Roger breathed: "That's got the mad Colonel! Any idea who he worked through at the factory?"

"Pretty certain to be Torrance or Grannett," Kimbell said. "Why don't you tackle Grannett's wife? Most of the factory trouble started in Grannett's department. Go after him."

Chapter Twenty

The Factory Again

The narrow street with terraced houses on either side was in the older part of Elling. At each end was a corner shop, and at each end a parked police car. Roger was aware of being watched by several policemen as he drove slowly to Grannett's house, Number 47. There were lights at some of the ground-floor windows; more lights upstairs. At Number 47 the only light was at the front door, which showed a pale glow from a light some distance inside. Outside it were two plain-clothes men.

One came to Roger, peered and recognised him, and saluted smartly.

"Has he come here?"

"No, sir."

"Who's in?"

"His wife and mother," said the plain-clothes man.

"When did you last speak to them?"

"Half an hour ago, sir, when we first arrived."

"Searched the place?"

"Oh, yes, sir. They let us look round."

"Garden?"

"We haven't overlooked a thing, sir, take it from me."

"Thanks." Roger got out and turned to the plainclothes man in the car. "Stay there, keep the radio on, and let me know if there's any flash about this job." He hurried to the little front door, and rang the bell, one of the battery type attached to the door; it sounded very loud. Almost immediately the glow of light showing against the glass panel became brighter, and there were footsteps in the passage. Then the door opened, and a woman whom Roger could see was youngish, and whose dark hair looked wavy and shiny against the light of a room beyond, stared at him.

"Mrs Grannett?"

"Yes," she said, and there was sharp disappointment in her voice, as if she had expected her husband.

"I'm sorry to worry you again. I'm Chief Inspector West of Scotland Yard, and I'd like a word with you."

She hesitated, then opened the door wider and stood aside.

"You'd better come in." She watched him as he did so, then closed the door. Another, older woman appeared at the end of the passage, and called out in a husky voice: "Is it Michael?"

"No, mum, I'll tell you the minute he gets in. It's another policeman."

Roger had an impression of a vigorous young woman who knew exactly what she was about, and of a frail, sad old lady. The older woman turned back to the lighted room, while Mrs Grannett stepped into a front room, switched on a light, and said: "We'll go in here, I don't want to upset mother any more than I must."

She was quite a beauty in her way. Small and sturdy and high-breasted, with a shapely waist. Gypsyish? That impression was probably caused by her dark eyes and black hair; there was something of the southern European about her. She moved briskly, too. Her gaze was searching, and Roger could imagine that she would take a lot of fooling.

"Well, what do you want?" she asked flatly.

He kept looking at her, but she didn't shift her gaze. Nor did she repeat the question. She knew quite well that he was trying to unnerve her; and was probably sure that he hadn't a chance.

At last, he said: "Where is he?"

"I haven't the foggiest idea," she declared, and her chin lifted an inch. "If I had, you wouldn't make me give him away."

Roger could believe that.

"I think you know where he would go," he said.

"Well, I don't know."

"Mrs Grannett," Roger said, "your husband escaped from us when being questioned about a serious crime. We have good reason to believe that another man, probably armed, intends to kill him. We want to make sure he can't.

He had worried her, but she surprised him by the question she asked.

"Who's the man after him?"

"Colonel Harrison."

"Oh!" she said, and the suspicion died out of her eyes. "Mike always said he was crazy. I still don't know where Mike is. I could make a guess, but I don't suppose that would be any good to you."

"Try it."

She said: "There are only two things in the world he's interested in, one is his home and family, and the other is that blasted factory. I don't know what you think he's done, but if you think he'd do anything to make trouble there, you're a pretty bad policeman."

Roger said: "That could be, too. Why did he hate Sir Ian Munro?"

"He's never hated anyone in his life."

"If you want to help him, the only way is with the truth," said Roger. His voice was very low; he did not want what he said to travel along the passage to the other woman's ears. "We're looking for him in connection with the murder of Sir Ian."

Mrs Grannett raised her hands sharply. Her eyes, shiny and very bright until then, seemed to go dull. She actually backed away from him, as if fending off some evil thing.

"I mean it," Roger said. "The murder of Sir Ian."

"It's impossible!"

"It happened tonight, soon after your husband went to Munro House. Why did he hate Sir Ian?"

Grannett's wife was breathing hard now, and Roger believed that she had some of the dead Munro's qualities; her husband's qualities, too. She would fight with everything she knew.

"I tell you he didn't hate anyone. He simply hated the things some of them stood for."

"It could be as important."

"He wouldn't kill anyone. Oh, he told me that you seemed to think he knew something about Roy's death, but that's crazy!" Her voice rose, and she was almost hysterical. "He loved Roy, nothing was too good for Roy. He mixed with the wrong set, but Mike was positive it wouldn't have come to anything."

"Did your husband try to break the association?"

"He—he wanted to, anyhow."

"Did he try to?"

"Yes!"

"Was young Woods a Communist?" When she didn't answer Roger gripped her arms and words were forced out of him. *"Was he?* Was your husband fighting a Communist group who meant to make trouble?"

"Yes," Mrs Grannett gasped. "Yes!"

So he had been right to assume that one man had not committed these crimes: it looked as if political fanatics who wanted only to make trouble had seized the chance, creating disaster, killing with that terrifying speed, and dovetailing all they did into the follies of both Sir Ian Munro and his son. There had been a confusion of motives to create confusion in investigation, but now – Roger was beginning to grasp the full significance of the situation.

All of this flashed through his mind after Mrs Grannett had gasped: "Yes!"

Now, he asked swiftly: "Did your husband have any particular association with Roy's friend, Woods?"

"No, I don't think so."

"With a man named Winn, or another named Pegnall?"

"No!"

"Did *Roy* have anything to do with them?"

"I don't think so," Mrs Grannett cried. "It's no use asking me, I just don't know."

"Did your husband have any association with Mr Torrance, the test driver?"

"No, but Roy did." The woman was on the point of tears. "Mr West, my husband has only one thing at heart, that's the good of the workers at Munro's. I'm as positive of that as that I'm standing here."

A sharp tap at the front door broke across her words. Roger hurried along the passage, and as the door opened, saw the plain-clothes man who had been standing by his radio.

"Just had a flash, sir. Colonel Harrison's been stopped at the factory. He says he believes Grannett is heading for the Powerhouse, meaning to blow it up."

It took fifteen minutes to reach the factory gates and five to find Harrison. He was with a group of Yard and Divisional men, and the factory police on night duty, at the Assembly Shop offices. In the great building itself, nothing seemed different from the daytime, except that there were fewer clerks in the offices.

Harrison was still ashen pale, his eyes glittered, he looked desperately ill. A crazed man? Would a madman buy up Munro shares so avidly? Would a madman take the chances which had been offered?

Remember how cunning the mad could be.

"I tell you Grannett's in the Powerhouse by now, we've got to get after him." Harrison's voice was clipped and toneless; as if defying the fierce brightness of his eyes. "I've always known he would rather see the factory in ruins than let the directors win. He knew he couldn't win, he knew Sir Ian was too strong."

Give Harrison his head, and he might lead to the whole truth.

"That's why he poisoned Sir Ian," Harrison went on, savagely. "He came to get his own way or to kill Sir Ian, the way he killed the others. And now he knows he can't get away with it, he'll bring ruin on the factory. That's why he'd head for the Powerhouse. If he can damage that seriously he can bring everything to a standstill, every man and every machine. For the love of God get moving, West! We've got to stop him. If he can get at the main control switches he can wreck the plant for months."

They reached the squat, square building, with its small windows and its single squat chimney, and Harrison, with two Divisional men alongside him, led the way to the main entrance. His voice rasped at the men on gate duty.

"Have you seen Grannett tonight?"

The man said promptly: "Oh, yes, sir, he's inside. Came in five minutes ago."

Chapter Twenty-One

The Powerhouse

Inside, the Powerhouse looked a mammoth place, stark and new, with a kind of beauty of line in the very severity of the design of the machines, the control panels, the dynamos. It reminded Roger of the control room in the Assembly Shop, but was on a much bigger scale. Here and there men in khaki overalls stood by the controls, or sat thoughtfully by them. There was little noise, except a deep, pulsating throb. A small man in a khaki smock came out of a door marked: management only, a ferret with beady eyes. He looked at the dozen men as if astonished, and said to Harrison: "Everything all right, sir?" He had a twangy voice.

"You seen Grannett?"

"No, sir."

"Well, he's here, and we want him."

"I'll use the loudspeaker and ask for reports," said the little ferret. "If he's here, he's probably at the main switchboard."

"We'll go there," Harrison said. "You put out a message for him." He turned and hurried down the wide stone passage between the great square steel structures which encased some of the engines; it was like a huge liner's engine-room, without the noise, the heat and grease, the pulsating machines.

Roger followed, and the others followed in turn, most of them looking about them as if overawed by the hugeness of the place. Their footsteps echoed, if Grannett was here he would have plenty of warning of their approach. Then suddenly a voice sounded, strangely hollow, and the echoes fell about their ears in waves.

"Attention all Powerhouse staff. If Michael Grannett is with you, please report to management at once. Will repeat that. If Michael Grannett is with you ..."

Harrison reached a junction of two wide passages, and turned left. Ahead lay a huge wheel, revolving so swiftly that it seemed not to be moving at all. Near it was a big control panel, with four men standing there on duty. A faint hum came from the wheel, that was all. Steps led downwards to an enormous, well-lit cavern, where the gigantic, pulsating machines were housed. Obviously this was the centre of the Powerhouse: that humming wheel represented the heartbeats of the factory.

There was no sign of Grannett.

One of the four men lifted a telephone and said quite clearly: "Main Switchboard Operator calling Management, Michael Grannett was here two minutes ago, and went down to the engine-room. Repeat. Michael Grannett ..."

Harrison broke into a run, but didn't get even a pace ahead of Roger or the Divisional men. He went hurtling past the man at the telephone. More noise came, too, mostly a deep throbbing note. Down there was the very bowels of the Powerhouse; all the machines, the pipes, cables, meters, and fittings which might have been expected above ground level were mostly underground. Here was life and death to the great plant.

And here, at the foot of the steps, was Michael Grannett.

He was standing quite still. Obviously he had expected something like this, and was quite prepared for it. He carried what looked like an old army revolver in his right hand.

"There he is!" screeched Harrison. "Kill him before he does more harm."

He snatched his right hand from his pocket and leaped at Grannett.

Roger saw a flash of something silvery as he snatched at Harrison's hand. A Divisional man grasped Harrison's other arm. Harrison tried to hurl the silvery thing away, but Roger caught it, felt it cold to his touch, and stood holding it.

It wasn't until an hour later that he knew it was nitroglycerine: enough to have wrecked the Powerhouse, and have blown him to smithereens.

"Why did you run away after Harrison was stopped at Munro's house?" asked Roger of Grannett.

Grannett said dryly: "I ran away from you, after Harrison gave me the chance. It looked as if they were determined to frame me."

"How did you think running away would help?"

"Believe it or not, I didn't trust the police to find out the whole truth," Grannett said. "I didn't trust anyone but myself. I was pretty sure that some of the Commies were stirring up trouble, but I couldn't see the Commies I knew as murderers. I had a pretty good idea that Old Lanky was a Commie, and might know more than he'd said. He does occasional night-shift work in the Powerhouse, so I went there. I put the fear of death into him," Grannett added, in a hard voice. "I told him I believed he'd pushed young Woods into that tunnel, and that I'd tip you off. He cracked."

"Where is he?" Roger asked.

"At the other end of the Powerhouse. Want to see him now I've done your job for you?" Grannett jeered. Then he said swiftly: "I take that back."

Lanky was a badly frightened man, now only too eager to talk. He had seen Harrison in the Paint Shop, near the tunnel, and had seen Woods there about the same time; that was the last time Woods had been seen alive.

"Why didn't you say so earlier?" Roger demanded. "Did Harrison bribe you?"

"No, Pegnall did. He said he'd push me in the tunnel if I didn't keep my mouth shut. Him and Winn, they've always done the dirty work for Torrance, and they've paid cash to other comrades who've done what he wanted."

"Such as paying you for fixing the heat in the tunnel so that a lot of bodies were overheated."

Lanky grunted: "They'd've given me a hell of a bad time if I hadn't, the Party didn't order that, the Party didn't know what was going on."

"I can believe it," Roger said. "Torrance always had a few Commies among his hero-worshipping crowd, didn't he?" He looked at Grannett. "I don't know this plant like you do, Mike, but I can put two and two together. Torrance always had his hero-worshippers. Some of them would do anything he told them. Roy was a hero-worshipper, and Torrance wanted him to make trouble for Malcolm Munro. Right?"

Grannett didn't answer.

Lanky said: "Yeh, Mike, that's right, Roy was out to make trouble all right."

"And he made it," Roger went on quietly. "He also knew that sooner or later you'd get the truth out of him, so Torrance killed him, as he'd served his purpose."

"Yes," agreed Grannett heavily. "I can see that's how it worked out."

"And Torrance used Pegnall to do a lot of other things," Roger added. "It would be Pegnall who bribed that front-office commissionaire to disappear when young Munro was attacked. It would be Pegnall who told Woods to fetch the hammer from the hiding-place, but Charley Coombs got there first. Who killed Charley? Was it Harrison?"

"I dunno," Lanky said.

"Is there one of Pegnal's men in the control tower at the Assembly Shop?"

"Yes," Lanky answered, and he was sweating. "One of the Commies."

It took half an hour to find the control-tower operator; only a few seconds to make him admit that Harrison had operated Panel 3, and killed Charley Coombs; and so great was the operator's fear of

Pegnall that he had lied, both about Harrison's position and his movement to touch the control button.

"He'd have fired me if I hadn't," the operator said, "sometimes I think he would have killed me."

"Once you realised that Harrison was mad, you could work the rest out," Roger said to Kimbell, a little later. "And he and Torrance worked together, each for his own ends, using Pegnall to bring the agitators to heel. The Communists knew nothing about the murders in advance. Mike Grannett realised that Harrison was crazy enough to try to wreck the Powerhouse, but Grannett says that he didn't think we'd believe that, so he went to stop Harrison if the attempt was made."

"Getting to like this chap Grannett, aren't you?" Kimbell asked.

By the time the talk with Kimbell was over, Malcolm Munro and Robert Amory were at the factory, with Tessa Lee. Roger watched as Grannett and the others met. They seemed more relaxed than he had known them, three men who could carry Munro Motors higher than it had ever been.

Janet would have liked the way Malcolm kept his arm round Tessa Lee's waist.

It was a month later that Malcolm and Tessa were married, very quietly, while Torrance and Harrison were still awaiting trial.

"I say, Dad," said Martin-called-Scoopy, about two months later, "don't you think it's a pity that Harrison and Torrance can't be hanged? Fancy letting them off with imprisonment for life."

"I'm glad one man in the family has some sense," Janet said, and smiled up at Roger from her sock-darning.

"I don't like hanging," announced Richard solemnly.

"That makes us two against two," said Roger, "so we'll call it even. And why don't you read some real news, Scoop, instead of all this shocking Old Bailey and police-court stuff. Didn't you see the piece about the Munro Mark 9? The export orders have gone past the twenty-million-pound mark."

The boys' eyes glistened.

"I wish we could have a Mark 9," sighed Richard, "and if you didn't earn one I'd jolly well like to know who did."

"You'd almost think they'd give you one, wouldn't you?" said Martin thoughtfully.

"All I can ever get for my job is pay and an easy conscience," Roger said; "anything else would be corruption."

"I wouldn't mind being corrupted just a little," declared Janet. "Did you see the other piece of news about Munro's, darling?"

"No. Don't say there's a little Malcolm on the way already!"

"What?" asked Richard.

"Shut up, you ass," said Martin.

"I didn't mean anything domestic," said Janet coldly. "I was thinking of business, which is more than you ever do. Michael Grannett has been appointed Works Manager. And Munro Motors shares have nearly doubled in value in the past few months. What a pity you didn't have the sense to put a few hundred pounds in them."

"I'm not exactly a wealthy man," said Roger humbly, "but I did manage to curb the expensive tastes of my wife and children and put a couple of thousand pounds away for a rainy day. I invested half of it in Munro Motors stock when the price fell heavily during the strike fears. I'm still not a wealthy man, but we could afford an evening at the pictures ..."

Janet was coming towards him, her eyes glowing. The boys looked at him with intense pride. He winked at them as Janet gave him as big a hug as she had for years.

When the boys had gone out, Janet said: "Darling, I hoped you'd say that you'd got promotion at last. Aren't you *ever* going to recognise how good you are?"

"I'm told that new appointments are due in a week or two," Roger said. "Keep your fingers crossed."

JOHN CREASEY

GIDEON'S DAY

Gideon's day is a busy one. He balances family commitments with solving a series of seemingly unrelated crimes from which a plot nonetheless evolves and a mystery is solved.

One of the most senior officers within Scotland Yard, George Gideon's crime solving abilities are in the finest traditions of London's world famous police headquarters. His analytical brain and sense of fairness is respected by colleagues and villains alike.

'The finest of all Scotland Yard series' – New York Times.

GIDEON'S FIRE

Commander George Gideon of Scotland Yard has to deal successively with news of a mass murderer, a depraved maniac, and the deaths of a family in an arson attack on an old building south of the river. This leaves little time for the crisis developing at home ....

'Gideon of Scotland Yard emerges as one of the most real working detectives in modern fiction.... A sympathetic and believable professional policeman.' - New York Times

JOHN CREASEY

THE CREEPERS

"The prisoner's hand was thin and bony ... And in the centre of the palm was a pinkish mark. It was the shape of a wolf's head, mouth open, fangs showing. Although it was what he had expected to see, Inspector West felt a twinge of repugnance a stab not unrelated to fear. It was the fifth time he had seen the mark of the wolf – the mark of Lobo."

A gang of cat burglars led by Lobo cause mayhem as they terrorize the city. They must be stopped, but with little in the way of evidence the police are baffled. Just how can Inspector West manage to do this in what is a race against time before more victims succumb?

"Here is an excellent novel of law enforcement officers, harried, discouraged and desperately fatigued, moving inexorably ahead under the pressure of knowledge that they must succeed to save human lives." - Cleveland Plain-Dealer

"Furiously exciting" - Chicago Tribune

"The action is fast, continuous and exciting" - San Francisco News

JOHN CREASEY

THE HOUSE OF THE BEARS

Standing alone in the bleak Yorkshire Moors is Sir Rufus Marne's 'House of the Bears'. Dr. Palfrey is asked to journey there to examine an invalid - who has now disappeared. Moreover, Marne's daughter lies terribly injured after a fall from the minstrel's gallery which Dr. Palfrey discovers was no accident. He sets out to investigate and the results surprise even him . . . .

"'Palfrey' and his boys deserve to take their places among the immortals." - Western Mail

INTRODUCING THE TOFF

Whilst returning home from a cricket match at his father's country home, the Honourable Richard Rollison - alias The Toff - comes across an accident which proves to be a mystery. As he delves deeper into the matter with his usual perseverance and thoroughness, murder and suspense form the backdrop to a fast moving and exciting adventure.

'The Toff has been promoted to a place of honour among amateur detectives.' – The Times Literary Supplement

Printed in Great Britain
by Amazon